Windward Manor

Donna Valenti Paterniti

WINDWARD MANOR

iUniverse books may be ordered through booksellers or by contacting:

iUniverse
1663 Liberty Drive
Bloomington, IN 47403
www.iuniverse.com
1-800-Authors (1-800-288-4677)

ISBN: 978-1-5320-6218-6 (sc)
ISBN: 978-1-5320-6219-3 (e)

Print information available on the last page.

iUniverse rev. date: 11/15/2018

In the small bay-town of Claiborne, a certain aura and mystery, held and surrounded Windward Manor.

Kristen Kendal returned to her home along the shore of the Chesapeake Bay determined to solve what her extensive research and curiosity could not appease.

The inquisitive Kristen meets the— fifth generation of Savage men to occupy the manor house.

Will she and the handsome Mitch Savage ever see eye to eye on the strange events... which encompass the manor?

And if they do... what will happen next?

Chapter 1

Set alone.. with windows shuttered for thirty-five years... a mystery... seized, and utterly captivated me... needed to be solved.

I walked along the shoreline. The aromas and sounds reminded me of my youth and good fortune to have grown up here. My return to live in the older home built in the late 1860's and in need of updated renovations would be a challenge for me. But it was home... where I belonged.

Always drawn to the manor house which held it's fascination most of my life... I walked closer to see if much had changed in the years I'd been absent. My extensive research on its history enthralled me.

With mom and dad in Arizona, and my return to Claiborne, the curiosity hadn't been resolved... I needed to continually search for answers.

The stroll along the shore took me closer to view the visible, widespread posterior of Windward Manor where the well-manicured lawn had been maintained for years... even to this very day.

A man worked effortlessly in the cool evening to keep from being caught in the heat of the day. I walked up the slight... grassy incline... from the water's edge to begin communications and moved closer to where he trimmed the inlaid stone walkway to acknowledge him... about the same time, he recognized me.

With a smile on my face I pushed back my hair, which had blown across my mouth... before I could say, "Alex North, I didn't know you were groundskeeper for the manor?"

He looked with recognition and turned off his trimmer, "Well hello, Kristen Kendal," was expressed with a surprised grin. "I've heard you were back in town. Funny thing, I was about to stop in your shop tomorrow to say hello. What made you give up your life in the big city to return here?"

I'm sure he'd heard, but none the less I'd repeat for him.

"My parents retired, turned the house and shop over to me. I couldn't pass it up. It was a sweet deal, live where I grew up, and have a place to work."

He put down the trimmer and walked towards me with a suggestive grin, "Well... it's what I'd heard... but wasn't sure those were the only reasons to bring you home."

I shrugged my shoulders, acted coy, and surprised, "What other reason would there be?" I asked.

I knew what he referred to. It had to be my ex-boyfriend Ethan Chester. He'd left Claiborne and followed me to San Francisco. What a mistake. We were too young— immature... and I wasn't in love with him. I felt like his mother, he expected me to do his laundry, and make decisions for him. We only lasted a month and he hightailed back home, but... my thoughts were... he was married, and I'd be safe from criticism. I'm sure our stories differed.

"No Alex... it was the main reason." Now I gave him a pleasant smirk. There may have been one small reason not worth my breath. "But of course I wanted to see if there had been any changes ... with Windward Manor. Much to my amazement I have to say, I never expected to see you here."

"Well, my grandfather took over the job of groundskeeper." Alex knelt on one knee, wiped his brow, and continued our conversation. "After the hurricane, which sank his boat in 2003, he retired. You remember when Isabel ripped through the town and all the damage from the storm surge?" "I do." My weight shifted onto one foot. "I was fourteen. Our home sustained damage, it could have been worse. I'd never guessed it was your grandfather who worked here. Always a bit leery of this place... even though I loved it... I never came close enough to actually see who maintained the property." I revealed.

"When Gramps took sick a few years back and my return from Afghanistan, I took over for him." Alex shrugged his shoulders. "It's no more than a pastime for me. A way to relax after a long day at the Pentagon." He stated.

"Wow. I'm not up on the latest news around town. Of course only home a month the shop needed preparation for the holiday weekend... I guess I've had my head buried in the sand. By the way... who over the last 35 years has paid for the upkeep on the outside of the manor?" I anticipated... finally there was someone who may know and be able to clarify who managed the estate all these years.

"You know, I'm not sure." Alex removed his hat and ran his fingers through his hair. "I do the work, but the check goes to my grandfather. I'd have to ask him. But my assumption is... a management company has been responsible for the administration... at least since Gramps began to work here. It's about all I know... but rumor has it... someone will soon remove the boards on the windows, and reopen the house before the end of summer. Don't ask me who, because I don't know this either."

Great... this was sensational news for me.

3

Enlightened and excited, I announced, "Well, you should get back to work before it becomes dark. It was good to see you again, Alex. Maybe I'll catch you the next time on my stroll." I said.

I turned to leave when Alex voiced, "By the way Ethan's been back about a year. You might want to look him up. He lives with his folks." He informed me.

"Thanks for the information, Alex." I replied.

He smiled... and waved goodbye.

The problem with a small town was... everyone expected you to marry within the city. They thought you should be satisfied to marry your high school sweetheart and raise a family. It wasn't for me. I wasn't in love with Ethan and never would be.. and for now I hadn't met anyone who held my attention since my broken engagement to Corbin... not interested anyway. The way I figured... I'd had more than enough to occupy my mind, with the shop, and renovations on my home.

With a portion of my funds the minor restorations had been completed. The outside paint had become blistered and peeled from the harsh weather attributed to life close to the water.

The clapboard's battered look needed to be sanded and repainted. The inside paint needed a change to give the house a fresh appearance. New colorful throw pillows and assorted pictures added to the freshness. These few effects made the home more my own. When business would become slow, other rooms would need to be updated... like the bathrooms, and kitchen. Thankful the house had been raised over the years to keep it above the storm surge... helped with the upkeep.

The shop was busy and tourism started out at its peak since Memorial Day. The town remained the same with the historic shops, and houses on Main Street, but the city itself had become more populated with stores, and hotels. Marinas and the restaurants associated with them were doing well.

As a graduate of Berkley, the bay area and its boats in Claiborne, began to remind me of why San Francisco felt like home.

I hated to leave my California home, but I'd now reside... not only where I grew up, fantasized about Windward Manor, but had the atmosphere of the bay in my life.

San Francisco had been perfect until my breakup from Corbin Callahan. It took me a few years to figure out he was a jerk. At least I'd be free of him in Maryland.

When the opportunity arose to come back home, have a place to call my own, a shop which would now belong to me... it was a no-brainer.

The flow of customers would help dictate the hours. To close early would allow me nightly walks along the shore. Since the shop had become busy... thoughts were we could use one more sales person... so I could enjoy those evening strolls.

Katie Horace was an employee. She'd recently graduated high school, was hired by my mother, and was perfect for the job. Her friend Brittany applied, had an interview, and would be given a work schedule. This would free me up to open shipments and arrange stock. I'd need both the girls for weekends through the fall.

Winter would be a slow time. My mother would remind me to put money earned away for a rainy day. I discovered it to be my specialty since I'd been on my own in San Francisco for eight years.

Ethan hadn't been seen or heard from since my return and I was not prepared to pursue him… the best way to handle the sticky situation, was stay to myself. He knew I was back in town and where to find me.

Chapter 2

My shop became a busy hub of old friends who'd drop by to see the changes made this season. It had once been a gift shop. For me I wanted it to be more. My inventory now included beach chairs, umbrellas, and so on. All things related to boats, the enjoyment of the beach, usual tourist postcards, and much more. One reason I'd need more help was to unload inventory and arrange displays for new items. This would continue on a daily basis.

After college many high school acquaintances, not necessarily friends... returned to Claiborne to open restaurants, marinas, food chains, pharmacies, and ice cream shops.

I didn't really have what some would consider a best friend in school... besides Ethan. I stayed mostly to myself... except for him.

We were friends since early childhood and later began to date by the eleventh grade.

My house was further away from school, but closer to Windward Manor. I spent most of my time lost in thought about the mansion's mystery than distressed about friends who lived on the other side of town... plus... I always had Ethan.

The town had a small, but quaint post office, which dated back to the early 1900's. The hardware store and antique shops on Main Street were all original structures. Most dwellings on the street became small businesses. Coffee shop, bakery, ice cream parlor, antique, and sandwich shops.

Main Street's buildings looked the same since I was a kid. The only thing which seemed to change was the paint. The different shades now correlated with the summer at the shore.

We weren't busy today. It was a good time to become better acquainted with Brittany. She reminded me of the small changes and goings-on in the town.

She'd laugh and proceeded to sweep the sand from the worn wooden floor.

We continued to work and wait on customers.

I couldn't help but think of Ethan. He'd ride his bike around a pond, through the small section of woods, which surrounded the manor, and be on the crushed oyster shell lane, which led to my house.

My home was close to what I referred to as a beach. It was easy to amble over to the manor house… or fish from our pier.

The North family, at least Alex's grandparents and parents, inhabited the largest house in the township. His father was our fire chief in the town's only firehouse.

There was also a small police station where Ethan's father remained Chief of Police and the local bank was in the best location… right next door.

I've seen and spoken to most of the small town's families and introduced to the new children and grandchildren… when they came to say hello. They'd wish me well as the shops proprietor.

Saturday early… I prepared to unlock the shop… my name was called. I'd turned to look—at first not sure—my thoughts said, yes… it was Ethan. He'd changed. Matured into a man. Not the lanky kid who followed me to San Francisco.

I smiled and said, "Ethan, good morning. Great to see you." The smile he gave me was the same one I'd remembered.

"Kristen, it's good to see you too."

He walked towards me, came closer, I sensed the fact he truly felt it was great to see me, and gave me a hug. A friendly one.

"Gosh, Ethan, you look wonderful. I guess life has been good to you?"

He pinched the end of his nose and gave me a smile as he released it. "You could say that. I returned home after my six years in the service and opened the Crab Shanty." His smile became brilliant when he said, "Best crabs in town."

This tickled my funny bone, it was more than likely the only place in town to buy crabs… and seafood.

"Someone mentioned the Crab Shanty, but I didn't realize you were the owner. Where are you located from here? I'll have to stop by. There haven't been crabs in my life since I've returned." I recalled.

"My place is off the alley by the marina's boardwalk." He said. "It's been given a name so tourists can find me." He sounded excited. "Crab Alley seemed an appropriate name… a street sign has been put in place."

"You know when my parents lived here and I was in San Francisco, they never relayed any of the town's news to me. Their thoughts were I'd never return and wasn't interested. I'd no idea you or Alex had been in the military. It's hard to imagine it was the best time to enter military life." I questioned.

He stood erect and looked serious, "Kristen, I had a lot

of growing up to do... I'll admit ... my sergeant became my mother, and my tour of duty turned me into a man."

I shifted my weight nervously, "Ethan, it seems so long ago when we parted ways. I'm sorry. I probably didn't handle our relationship in the right manner, but being young and independent at the time..."

Now he laughed, "I hear you're still independent. You've never married I'm told."

"Nope, never found the right guy." I replied with a smile.

"Hate to break this to you— but there aren't many new faces around here, so... good luck." He joked.

"Thanks, Ethan, but right now until I'm settled... a man is the furthest thing from my mind."

He gave me another quick hug, "Go... get yourself set for the day. We do need to catch up. Stop by tonight on your way home. I'll save you a dozen jumbo crabs. Maybe you'll invite me back to your place to eat them and we can talk... I'll bring the beer?" He anticipated with a smile.

"Oh!... Okay." I was surprised he'd asked. "I guess it's time to get caught up on this city since it's now my home."

We said goodbye, he walked off towards the marina and the Crab Shanty. He'd bring crabs and beer to my house when he closed for the night.

After I thought about it, maybe it wasn't the right decision. I liked Ethan and always would, but it ended there.

Chapter 3

It was 9:15 p.m., I heard the knock on the door… it was Ethan. He called when he'd left the Crab Shanty to make sure I'd be home. I closed the shop at exactly 9:00 p.m. and with Katie's help we were able to leave on time.

The day's cash was counted, it correlated with the amount shown on the computerized register, the deposit was made at the local bank's updated night drop, and I was home before Ethan's expected arrival.

I opened the door to his pleasant face and the smell of steamed crabs.

My hands empty and ready, I said, "Let me take the beer."

He handed me the six pack, was led through the kitchen, and then out onto the screened-in porch.

"How about you spread newspaper on the picnic table?" I asked.

"Okay. I can handle it." He said with a smile and set the bag of crabs down.

"Great. While you spread the paper, I'll get the mallets, knives, and a cooler with ice to put the beer in." Was my response.

He nodded when I walked past him.

Upon my return to the porch with the cooler and utensils we'd need, I turned on the porch fan attached to the overhead light. Two citronella candles, brought from the shop were set on the table. They were lit and I excused myself to dress more appropriately for— crabs and beer.

I appeared in a comfortable outfit and he responded, "Well, I think we're ready to dig in."

Seated across the table from him I said, "Thanks, Ethan. This was a great idea. So tell me, how's business, and what besides crabs do you sell?"

He looked up from cracking a claw to tell me, "When I opened last year I applied for a liquor license... and you can see I've received the okay to sell beer. We handle the catch of the day, clams, oysters, soft crabs, the shrimp come in from the Gulf, and whatever seafood we can get our hands on. The area's watermen... keep me in a fresh supply of fish." He paused long enough to pop a piece of claw meat into his mouth. "I decided to add a four season, outside deck to make room for the locals, and tourists to have somewhere other than their hotel or car to eat crabs." It will be an eat in, or carry out restaurant." He boasted.

After I took a healthy sip of cold beer and set the bottle down, I said, "Great idea. Claiborne can certainly use it. I've seen the large restaurants which have cropped up outside of town in the marinas. Great insight on your part, Ethan."

"Well... I need to earn an income for my family." He replied before he sipped on his beer.

I'm sure he saw the shocked expression on my face. "Congratulations on the family. I didn't know. Is your wife okay with this get-together?" I queried.

"Jeanette's... on tour in Afghanistan for a few more months, then she'll be home for good with me and our daughter Cory, who's five. We both miss her."

I took a mallet to a claw, but focused on him "I bet you do, how long have you been married?" I probed.

"Three years. I met Jeanette before my tour to Afghanistan while we were both stationed at Fort Bragg. Cory was two when we married. I've adopted her." He handed me a paper towel. "Jeanette knew she'd have to serve a second tour of duty before she finished her time and there was no one to take care of Cory. She wasn't the main reason we'd married, but was the sensible one. Jeanette is an army nurse." He informed me.

He seemed quite proud and handed me another crab. "She went to school on the army and had to sign on to pay back her education." He opened a beer. "You know, the ROTC program and had to serve at least eight years. She'll be finished the first part of September. Her career began when she finished high school. Of course there were no thoughts of a baby, but it has worked out well for her... and for me. Cory is such a sweetheart... like her mom."

"I'm so happy for you, Ethan. I'd hoped I hadn't ruined your life."

He laughed, "I thought maybe I've ruined yours since you haven't found the right guy."

I had to inquire, "Who has Cory when you work and while you're here?"

"My mom." He said. "I was on tour when Jeanette was sent to Afghanistan and neither of us were available. Mom said she'd be happy to take on the responsibility of grandmother until I returned, but she's not able to give her up. We've lived with my parents, but now the business has become more profitable. We'll move into our new home on the outskirts of town when Jeanette returns.

"Your wife must be so excited?" I responded.

"We both are... and Cory can't wait to have her mother back with us."

"It must be hard on Cory... and you?"

"Yes. But I stay busy and my parents spoil her. Of course I spoil her too. You'll have to meet her." He said nonchalantly.

I paused to look right at Ethan with my head cocked and a thank you for the invitation, "I'd love too. You'll have to bring her by the shop or tell your mom to stop by with her."

Our conversation continued with ease and Ethan asked me questions about San Francisco. I went into detail about my life, my job as a history teacher, and the ex-fiancé.

"Ethan, I sense you're upset for me because of the way and why… Corbin and I split?" I inquired.

"Of course I am, Kristen. He sounds like a real idiot. Don't forget you were my best friend since we were kids."

I gave him a smile. The discussion carried on through the swallows of cold beer and the enjoyment of the Old Bay seasoned steamed crabs. But then he raised an eyebrow and asked, "Are you still obsessed with Windward Manor. Before you left for San Francisco you swore you would find out what happened to the woman who lived there and the mystery behind Mitchell Savage."

I didn't raise my head while I continued to pick at the crab I was engrossed in, then answered quietly, "Yes. I've done extensive research on the family, but it stops with Mitchell and the missing woman." I raised my head to look at Ethan. "The boards will soon come off the windows and I'm drawn to the house, but even more so… since my return." I claimed.

"You need to let it go, Kris. It's an empty old house." He stated as a concerned friend.

"Yes, but it's full of secrets and I will find out… I have to know … why, what and how, Ethan. I have no explanation for the reason behind my fascination, or passion for the mansion…" I raised the bottle of beer to my lips… the cold reassured me of my thirst to solve the mystery.

Ethan said no more and the subject was changed

We'd finished most of the crabs, which were delicious, and planned on another get together... I hoped it didn't include more questions on my special interest.

Ethan suggested, "How about the next time we take this to the new deck at the Crab Shanty?"

"Sounds good to me," I replied.

My assumption was not to cause a stir of gossip for the town's people.

Chapter 4

The shop and I stayed busy. August was almost upon us. I'd had the opportunity to meet Cory, see Mrs. Chester, and the Chief again. I also met Jeanette on Skype.

Every Sunday evening, I'd sit on the new deck, eat crabs or other fresh seafood with the Chester's, Ethan, Cory, Alex North, and his wife Ava.

Ava and I became friends. She wasn't a local girl. Alex and she'd met while he was in the service, married a few years ago before his discharge. She taught in the local elementary school, for now she seemed to enjoy summer. School would start soon. She appeared more than ready to begin a new year.

I liked her wit and pleasantness. She and Alex were a great couple. Her blonde hair and fair skin didn't allow for her to be out in the sun often. Although they had a boat and could relax onboard, she was fortunate it had a canvas awning.

A discussion took place about how I should take time off.

"Kristen, I think you need to go with us one day, or maybe an evening for a boat ride, dock at one of the marina's, and eat in one of the newer restaurants." She invited.

I could eat here at Ethan's place, but the boat ride would be nice. "I'll think about it." I said. "Usually by the time I get home from the shop on the weekends I'm tired and want to relax and watch the sunset on the bay."

Some evenings when the sun made its descent... it appeared like a large orange beach ball ready to plummet into the water. It cast its auburn glow over the steel grey of the bay—for what one might expect as favorable for the next day.

Most evenings I went for my walk along the sandy portion of the shore, from my house to Windward Manor, shoes in hand, bare feet in the water... I'd rest on the grassy knoll of Windward's luscious lawn. There, with the sun's decline, sounds of water lapping upon the shore, the smell of the bay, and cool of the evening, *after the heat of the day...* I'd fantasize about what life was like back when the house first came into existence.

I thought about my research on the manor. Throughout its crop producing years, a channel had been dredged to receive larger vessels for outbound shipments from the manor's crops of tobacco. Since the 1930's the house had been added onto to create a massive domain. No one knew why, but by 1980 the house had been boarded up and the land which surrounded it had been sold. It now sat on fifteen—abandoned acres.

Would I ever know what happened and why this lovely place had no one to share in its beauty? I could only wonder what it would be like to live in the gorgeous estate, which held so much fascination for me of the unknown.

I pondered what the interior may be like. Soon I'd be able to see since Alex said the boards on the windows would be removed. For now I could only envision what the inside of the house was like from the sense I'd been there long ago.

Tonight I sat longer than usual and the mosquitos nipped at me. I'd have to continue my evening with a cool drink on my screened in porch... including a citronella candle to ward off the bugs which came along with summer... and the bay.

My mind continued to focus on the manor, love, life, and work... it never seemed to take a break. My walks helped to relax me and maybe a boat ride would be good and a nice idea. I'd talk with Ava tomorrow and set a date for a Sunday sunset or one sundown during the week. I hoped Ethan wouldn't become upset with me if a Sunday evening worked out better for the ride. It seemed he enjoyed the time spent with us when we patronized his restaurant. Thoughts were when we gathered on the deck at the Crab Shanty... it helped pass the time while he waited for Jeanette's return. Maybe a week night... would be better for a cruise.

My cell phone rang and I tossed the thought from my mind ... I saw the call was from Corbin. I didn't really want to answer it?

But I did.

"Hello?"

"I didn't expect you to take my call, Kristen. It's been months, thought maybe I may have crossed your mind once or twice, since you left?"

I'm sure he could sense by my tone. I was annoyed, "Actually Corbin, I've been busy. The last time you crossed my mind... I don't think you'd want to know what my thoughts were."

"I'm sorry for the way things turned out for us. I didn't mean for it to end this way or at all. I didn't mean to hurt you."

The candle extinguished, I headed into the house with the conversation.

"Hey, you know what, Corbin... I'd rather hurt... than feel

nothing and I don't feel a thing for you. Maybe I never did, because I find if I can look back and it doesn't interest me anymore... than it was never there to begin with."

"You sound bitter, baby. I planned to stop by and check on you. I'm on my way through Maryland and hoped you'd give me a tour."

I didn't need him now or his... *I'm sorry.*

He was sorry. He was a cheater and a liar. "Corbin ... now is not a good time for me. Summer is hectic here on the bay and my shop keeps me busy ... even on weekends. I wouldn't have time for you."

"Okay, just thought I'd ask... since I'm so close... your loss."

My loss... it was my loss... a lot of time, energy, and sleep that's what I lost. "Oh... I think you have it wrong... it's your loss. Good bye."

I turned my phone off, not simply to end the call, but off. Now I knew I wouldn't be able to sleep tonight. Why did I let him beat me down? When I cancelled the engagement... at the time it seemed to be the worst thing in my life I'd ever had to do... and it was.

I'd never let him know the humiliation and pain felt after he'd cheated on me. I've tried to forgive him, but couldn't get back the sensation of love, and knew a life together would never work. Headed forward... I wouldn't think about him and could not let myself cave now.

Why'd I answer the phone?

It was time to call it a night. I'd turn my phone back on when I was ready for bed and settled upstairs. Maybe it was the right time to place a call to my mother.

Chapter 5

What a restless night I'd had. I spoke with my mother and father, but didn't tell them about the call from Corbin. I told them about Ava and how we'd become friends, the get together on Sunday evenings with Ethan, and the shops progress. It was a good conversation, but then I had the rest of the night to think about Corbin. I needed to put him out of my mind.

Today would be busy. I planned to restock the shelfs and displays... I was tired from my thoughts, and lack of sleep. It would be a two cup, coffee morning for me.

Brittany would be in the shop by 10:00 a.m. and Katie would come on at two. Even though I unlocked my door by 9:00 a.m. and closed at 5:00 p.m. it would be a long day for me.

Midmorning was slightly busier than first anticipated, but between Brittany and myself, we could handle it. I'd still be able to restock.

She went on break first since she'd be off when Katie came on for the duration of the afternoon. I'd order my lunch from the sandwich shop across the street upon her return.

A veggie sandwich today would be enough for me and a bottle of water.

I took my lunch to the small lunch room in back of the shop where the door was open to the sounds, scent, and breeze from the bay… it couldn't help but make lunchtime pleasurable. Sometimes I'd sit outside at the picnic table, able to hear, and see if the girls in the shop needed my help.

The bell over the door rang and alerted me someone had entered the store. I'd forgo my lunch if it became busy. Mondays weren't usually hectic except for the additional inventory to be placed on the shelves. I thought Britt would be okay… but then I heard a voice I knew all too well.

"Hi. Is Kristen in?"

It was Corbin, why didn't he take no for an answer?

Of course Brittany said yes and called to me.

I had to go.

It had been months since I'd seen him and his appearance always took me by surprise. He was tall, perfect in every way, pleasant to gaze upon with his hazel eyes, blond hair, and of course he appealed to me now as he had before I knew better than to become involved with him. He wasn't just a snack, but the whole meal… so I thought.

He displayed his attractive smile when he saw me, *"Well if Mohammad won't go to the mountain, the mountain must come to Mohammad."*

I didn't want to appear overjoyed to see him… because I wasn't. "I told you I was busy." I took a deep breath and shook my head. "Why are you here?"

"I've been concerned about you. Is there somewhere we can talk?"

"I was about to have lunch…"

"Good, may I join you?" He asked.

"There's a sandwich shop across the street. I suggest you find lunch there."

"Come on Kristen, can't we talk." He seemed to plead.

"Okay then, I'll watch you eat and you can listen to what I have to say."

"Corbin, enough has been said. It's over, done... got it?" I responded.

I picked up my lunch and moved out back to the picnic table so Brittany wouldn't overhear our conversation.

I think I'll take sometime today to see if Kristen will help with a surprise welcome home party for Jeanette. She should be at lunch and we can talk.

Brittany saw me enter the shop, she seemed busy straightening miscellaneous items.

"Is Kristen at lunch?" I asked.

She responded, "Some guy... I think his name is Corbin... is outside with her at the picnic table."

I saw through the hallway which led outside. Kristen stood by the table. Her lunch hadn't been touched. She and Corbin were deep in discussion.

Brittany said Kristen didn't look happy. I knew the story and I'm sure she wasn't. The only way to help would be to intervene. I caught Kristen's attention. Winked, removed my wedding band, walked through the back door to where she stood, and kissed her lips lightly.

"Hey, sweetheart, want to go to lunch? For some reason all I seemed to get on your phone was your voice mail. Who's your friend?" I turned and reached my hand out to Corbin. "Hi. I'm Ethan Chester. Kristen's fiancé, are you friend or foe?" I laughed. *This was said … to break the ice.* I placed my arm around Kristen's waist and felt her body tremble.

She smiled up at me and said, "Past friend. I've told you about him…. Corbin Callahan."

Ethan was tall and lanky years ago, but no longer. Now powerfully built, stood a few inches above Corbin, and was a good looking guy. He had on a short sleeve tee-shirt, the cotton sleeves hugged his bi-ceps, and accentuated his muscular build. There was no fat… pure muscle.

Corbin was also an attractive man, but smaller frame and more of the business type… although he was physically fit for his height and stature. He kept himself in great shape by going to the gym where he could always find himself a girl… to cheat on me.

A look of surprise was read on Corbin's face I wanted to kiss Ethan to death. *Thank you Lord.* He couldn't have come at a better time.

Ethan answered his own question. "I was hopeful it was friend not foe, but I think I might have to put you in the foe category. Maybe you should say goodbye now." Ethan looked at me, "Kristen would you want to say goodbye to Corbin, or were you two involved in a friendly conversation. By my estimation the exchange didn't sound friendly?" Ethan alleged and stood close to me his arm around my waist.

I felt brave and said, "I think our chat is over, for lack of a better word. Thanks for the visit, Corbin, enjoy the East Coast."

He turned, walked towards the door, and out through the front of the shop.

I prayed he'd never find out Ethan was married as he hugged me a bit tighter. I buried my face in his shoulder for a second before I said, "Thank you. Your timing couldn't have been better. I didn't want Corbin to upset me. The shock of his phone call was enough last night and then he showed up out of the blue after I told him I didn't want to see him... it's left me a little stunned. So why am I so lucky my BFF dropped by?" I asked with relief.

I watched Ethan place his ring back on his left hand and give me a big smile.

"I've never taken this off in three years, don't tell Jeanette." He implored.

"She'd have been proud of how you saved a friend's butt just now... but it's our secret." I promised.

Chapter 6

I ate part of my sandwich while Ethan talked. By the time he finished he'd made me feel better about Corbin's visit. Then he asked if I'd help him plan Jeanette's welcome home party.

"I'd love to. Where will this surprise take place?" I inquired.

Ethan appeared more relaxed when asked since, Jeanette was the subject of interest, "The best place would be the fire hall. I'd like to dress up the hall and maybe have fancier food. This is why I need a ladies touch. Ava will help, but she'll be back to school and I'm not sure with papers to grade how much help she'll be. I know you're busy, but as the season slows, so will the tourists. Not that I want to see you make less money, but it does happen." He added.

"I need to get back to work, but I promise... especially since I owe you..." I began to laugh and said, "I'd love to help and will take a look at the fire hall again, it's been a long time since I've been there. I'll see what we can do to spruce up the place. Dessert should be Smith Island cakes. We'll need a headcount for food, a caterer, and of course invitations."

"Sounds good. Thank you for the help. Mom is always busy with Cory and her activities. I don't want to add more to her list. I'll be in touch. By the way Corbin was a jerk... is a jerk. That was a *BS* line he tried to feed you. Worse one I've ever heard. You're better off without him."

I chuckled, "Thanks, Ethan, I'm aware of this... I didn't like how he wanted to make his wandering eyes my fault, he's the one with the problem. Like I said before... good riddance."

Ethan had a frown on his face, "Is this how you felt about me when you sent me home?"

I shook my head, "No... even though we didn't stay in touch I knew we'd always be family. We were good friends far too long and I think we may have interpreted it as being in love. You know what love feels like since Jeanette... am I right?"

"Yep, you hit the nail on the head. I do love you, but I'm not in love with you... big difference." He said with a smile.

I gave him a hug and said, "Yes, big difference. Thanks for the rescue. Maybe tonight, I'll come to the Shanty with paper and pencil... we can come up with a plan. Thanks again, Ethan."

"Okay, I'll see you later," He sounded happy and whistled a tune on his way out of the shop.

Back to work with thoughts of a welcome home party and a goodbye for good to Corbin. I hoped Brittany hadn't overheard too much of the conversation. My mind centered on if both the girls were able to handle the store a few hours while I took time to look at the hall, think about food, and decorations. We had less than three weeks to get this party together.

I settled down enough to look over my new inventory and checked to see how much more we'd need before the Labor Day tourists hit our little town. I think the Crab Shanty, and the new marina began to draw a crowd, plus the new shops on Main Street helped.

It was time for Brittany to leave and Katie to come on for her four hour shift. The girls alternated hours and would have to give me their school schedule when they both registered for College, not far from here.

While it was quiet, I asked the girls about their help to handle the store for a good portion of a day for me to work on the surprise party.

They looked at one another and replied, "Sure not a problem for us."

It surprised me when Brittany said, "I thought it was nice of Ethan to help you today."

"Yes it was." Of course I asked, "What did you hear?"

I explained the friendship Ethan and I shared again after all these years, and to please not let the story go any further than the shop. "I'm not worried about a rumor being started about Ethan and me… but because I don't want Corbin to find out I'm not engaged." I stated.

"I understand, Kristen." She stood with her hands on her hips and said with a frown, "So… was he an example of what men are like from San Francisco?"

Now we both began to laugh. It had been said seriously. I hugged her to me and said, "Sadly… but truth is… you may run into creeps like him anywhere."

Katie wasn't sure what was going on. We gave her a brief rundown of the day.

I found it a joy to work with these two young ladies, educate them on what a good relationship between a guy, and a girl was supposed to be like.

We had a few good laughs. I encouraged them if they ever needed to talk and didn't know how to approach their mother's, I'd be glad to give advice, but after today I'd be ready to receive it as well.

Katie and I'd been busy. The question remained, why did people stay on the water until almost dusk... then come to shop for the next day's supplies—right before we closed? I was glad this day, and the confrontation with Corbin were behind me... anyway I hoped.

I went home to change into more casual clothes, flip flops, then to the Crab Shanty with a notebook, pencil, to eat dinner, and have a cold beer. I hoped since the town seemed quiet, maybe Ethan would be free to start work on the party.

"How about a crab cake and an ear of corn?" Ethan asked as he leaned on the counter.

"Sounds good. I didn't eat much of my lunch." I replied.

We sat and made an outline on what needed to be done.

"I'll take a look at the hall tomorrow. Will you have it catered? I think it would be nicer and we'll be able to enjoy ourselves."

"I think you may be right, Kristen. But by who?" He asked.

"I'll ask mom about a caterer, she has friends in the nearby towns and they would know who would be the best. We'll choose a menu."

Ethan suggested he and Alex take care of the bar setup and beer. Opinion was Smith Island cakes would be a great choice for dessert. Their eight to fifteen thin layers, filled with wonderful frosting would be perfect. They had serval varieties to choose from. We should try each variety once we had a handle on the number of guests... maybe a few of each flavor.

The party was planned, a caterer found, menu in place, invitations sent, cakes ordered and the decorations would soon be finalized. The party was arranged and I watched in earnest as the boards on the windows of the Manor house were removed.

I couldn't have been any happier for Ethan knowing his wife was on her way home and out of Afghanistan. She was safe, I was happy for me, because I hoped to soon discover the mystery behind Windward Manor.

Chapter 7

M y normal practice each evening after work would be to take my walk along the shore to see what may have been accomplished during the day on the mansion. One evening I became aware of a light in an upper window.

Although it was faint, there couldn't possibly be electric in the house. I tried to brush it off with thoughts it was a reflection from the upcoming moon as the sun began to set.

The following evening I noticed there was no way to complete my walk. More than a few pieces of equipment were parked on the gracious lawn close to the water's edge. Pilings had been driven into the sandy portion of the beach. This was the early stage of a pier.

Could it be to fish from or dock a boat?

There was equipment to dredge, which could mean a larger vessel would be able to dock and what may have been dredged over a hundred years ago wouldn't be sufficient for today's boats.

The supports I saw were huge and laid on the once, well-manicured lawn... now a muddy mess.

Almost furious with the thought of what might take place

if the manor had been sold… but someone in town would have heard, and rumors would fly—there weren't any… at least none I was aware of.

Who could I ask, Alex? No. He'd been removed from his job at the mansion, or actually his grandfather was no longer employed by the management company to maintain its property.

Prayers for this house. It couldn't be turned into a B&B or a hotel with its own docking facilities?

Further up the lawn… more earth would be excavated, and the magnificent yard destroyed.

I wanted to cry.

For years the house had been a mystery to me, but at least it was at peace, now it's been torn apart.

Tonight again— the soft glow of light in the upstairs window could be seen.

Decision made… my next free evening I'd travel the wooded road to view the house from the front and see if I could find someone who might tell me… what was to take place.

Until such time, I needed to return home, finish my work on the table decorations, and other adornments for Jeanette's party on Saturday.

The hall wasn't extremely large. There would be a hundred guests, mostly local families and their children. This was a family party since Cory was included.

Ethan would pick Jeanette up at the airport. Her plane would land about 4:00 p.m. and they should be close to home at least by 5:45. Party was at six.

I'd closed the shop today to decorate.

The ceiling in the hall was plain white, with new recessed lights, which made it easier to string small clear bulbs close together to shed an ambience of elegance when the ceiling fixtures were off.

At each electrical outlet around the hall... stood a four foot tall... tin umbrella stand complete with bare tree branches, lit with the same clear lights.

Since it was September, red clay pots with multi-colored mums embedded in each... were used as centerpieces.

The ten round tables, with the palest shade of yellow coverings, were surrounded by ten white folding chairs. Tables set up along the wall for appetizers, food, and desserts were also tastefully decorated.

Ava approached me, "Kristen, what else do we need to do?"

"We're all set." I responded with conviction. "The caterer will begin to display the appetizers at 6:00 p.m., even if Ethan is not back from the airport. The food will be served not long after their arrival. This will give them the opportunity to greet everyone. I'm glad I thought about music and was able to find a DJ for tonight. He's set-up and ready."

"Kristen, what did Ethan tell Jeanette to surprise her? I'm sure she will be tired and would like to change if she knew there was a party." Ava inquired.

"The way I understand... Jeanette knows she's coming straight to the hall. She thinks Cory has a dance recital at 6:00 p.m., or Ethan would have planned the party for later, and given her time to change. Cory knows the part she's to play... I hope... because Ethan has practiced with her on what she needs to say to her mother if asked about the recital. She's dressed appropriately in her ballet costume and slippers. But her recital isn't for a few more weeks. He's to call when Jeanette's plane lands. He'll ring my phone once, when they turn onto Main Street."

The surprise welcome home party was a hit.

It went off without a hitch. Jeanette was surprised and like Ava said, Ethan and she were meant for one another. I knew I'd like her.

Having the preparation for the party to take my mind off of Corbin's visit had been wonderful. My assumption he'd returned to the West Coast left me with the sense of security and more relaxed... to check on the activities at Windward Manor. Now this was another story. I've no idea what transpired there besides—disorder.

Chapter 8

I've never seen so much equipment in one area before. My father built a wall and dune, after the hurricane, which had done a lot of damage to our property, and home. There was equipment, piles of sand, and rocks to create a barrier, but not anywhere close to what was up-to-the-minute at Windward Manor.

The most puzzling thing of all was after I probed and questioned the contractors, no one knew who owned the property or what it was to be used for... which was another mystery. Why would they put in such a long, wide pier... and swimming pool?

I asked if the electric was on in the house since the light was seen in the evening.

The gentleman I talked to shrugged his shoulders and said, "The interior work is being done with the use of generators until the wiring is updated."

I asked, "Have you been inside the house?"

"No. My job is outside." Then he asked, "Why do you want to know?"

I explained about the light, but maybe it was a reflection?

"Ma'am, I don't know what you saw, but there's been some gossip about weird activities inside. All I can say is I'm glad I'm out here."

"What kind of events?" I was more than plain curious. I stepped closer to the contractor. He removed his hat and scratched his bald head.

"They're not sure if it's vandals or what, but they can't seem to finish a job. When they return the next day things have been changed or moved. Crazy stuff like this. Who knows maybe the house is haunted or has a spirit who doesn't like change."

I hadn't been by the house before the last few sunsets, but this evening I was going to take a walk through the trees and see if anyone was there. The contractors and crew had gone for the day. If I didn't see anyone—I'd snoop around with hope the owner would be here, I'd introduce myself, and ask questions. I approached the house, didn't see a car or any sign of life, human or otherwise. Maybe until the new construction was complete, the owner would not be available.

Being inquisitive for so many years, I found myself moving closer, and closer to a window to peer inside. Work had been done on the inside as well... because when I asked about the light... I was told more than was needed to know.

I trusted there wouldn't be ghosts or spirits to chase me away.

From what I could perceive through a few windows, there were paint buckets, stacks of new wood, tarps spread around the rooms to paint, and be refurbished.

One of the contractors stated the kitchen was being remodeled and a gourmet kitchen would replace the old. Bathrooms were to be updated, also the electrical, plumbing, and heat. Air conditioning would be added.

I couldn't imagine the restorations on this house to be

anywhere near complete this year. If they were lucky the outside may be finished before the cold and rainy fall hit the small bay town, but the inside would take the contractors through the winter... this was my perspective.

It turned dark earlier since we were into the end of September. I needed to turn around and start for home. It would have been easier to travel along the shore, but there was considerable disruption and no clear way from the manor to my portion of beach. I'd have to go through the woods and down the lane. It would be dark before I reached my house.

Cautiously I walked home. The renovations on Windward Manor were extensive. Whoever owned the manor must have a great job or really deep pockets.

I turned to look back at the house in its quiet location... the slight glow of light could be seen. It felt eerie. My pace quickened through the now dusk twilight as it began to turn into night.

Eventually I'd meet the new owner, but before it ever happened, there was a lot of work to be done. I had restoration work to complete on my home, but what the owner of the manor started... when it was completed... would be monumental.

Finally I reached home, quickly entered, tried to think positive thoughts about Windward Manor, and prayed there were no vandals close by. My house sat alone... away from town. I'd rather think the spirit of Mitchell would oversee the type of renovations being completed to his home.

Chapter 9

Jeanette was the perfect fit for Ethan and a wonderful mom. We'd all become friends. I was fortunate enough to be included with Ava, Alex, Ethan, and Jeanette.

I'd had more time away from the shop since the tourist season was about over, but there was still quite a bit of weekend activity while the weather stayed unseasonably warm for October.

Ethan and Jeanette prepared to move into their new home. Ava and I were to help. The three of us took a day to shop at the outlet stores. Our conversations were based on the latest gossip in town.

Neither of them could understand my eventual dream of a life in Windward Manor, finding out the deep dark secret of why, and what had happened so many years ago when the house was boarded up. Unfortunately things didn't look good for me to discover answers... or to live in the manor. Of course we'd laugh about my ridiculous hopes and dreams.

I continued my almost daily walks to the front of the manor with expectations to see someone, ask whether the house was to be a B&B, a hotel or someone's residence, and who… would reside here?

Very early one evening… before it turned dark by five o'clock… and with desperation in my steps… I walked to the mansion. There… a car was parked close to the house in the circular drive. I felt an excitement which was extremely difficult for me to control. It was even harder for me to contain the sense of uncertainty as to what had taken place in this house. I walked to the opened front door… knocked seriously on the doorjamb and shouted, "Is anyone home?"

A man whose back was towards me… turned around slowly and in an instant my breath caught in my throat. I didn't want him to notice how his appearance startled me. I don't think I've ever seen, or met a man with his more than impressive good looks. He had the most amazing blue eyes and they were focused directly upon me.

"May I help you?" He asked indifferently.

It certainly wasn't said in a friendly manner. But I wasn't about to let it deter the question which had plagued me.

I stepped further inside, "Are you the owner?" I asked.

His response was, "Who wants to know?"

Muddled and self-conscious at his response I timidly said, "I'm sorry. I'm Kristen Kendal… a neighbor… the one whose property borders to the left."

He took a step closer. I didn't think I'd be able to exhale… my breath stuck somewhere between my chest, and my throat.

"So, how may I help you?" Was his overly stated reply.

He hadn't introduced himself, but I continued. "I wonder… who will occupy this house? I've loved it since I was a young girl, felt badly it's been uninhabited for so long, and could only speculate what it looked like on the inside. Its outward appearance is magnificent."

Another step closer... I could inhale his scent of cologne, his eyes mesmerized me. Dear Lord... he was striking. His blue eyes, high cheekbones, straight nose, and his almost jet black hair... he had to be the finest, most handsome man, I'd ever laid eyes on. The shadow of his evening beard along his jaw... gave him a dangerous look... which made him much more... than simply attractive to me.

He spoke— but even though his voice was gentle it held a quality of authority. He gave a slight smirk when he said, "You must be the intrusive neighbor... who has bothered the construction crew."

I wasn't sure how to react to him, his looks had me mystified, but his manner was insufferable. Stunned, I didn't know what to say, needed to excuse myself, and walk away.

But I couldn't.

He stared. His eyes penetrated clean through to my soul. I've fantasized for so long about this house... I'd forgotten it wasn't a fairytale... and all was not required to turn out with a happy ending.

My hands in front of me clasped tightly together... I finally found my voice, "I'm sorry to have disturbed you. I guess the anticipation to see this house brought back to life after so many years... I... didn't think..."

I turned to leave. He said no more. Tears stirred behind my eyelids and were anticipated. Before I reached the front walk they'd fallen upon my cheeks. It was almost dark and with my now outpour of tears... for being such a dolt. I began to stumble through the woods, and lost the path I was to follow.

I reached my home totally distressed and couldn't seem to stop the flow of waterworks, which had manifested.

Why had I ever thought the dreams of a young girl, would ever come true? I'm so foolish and to think at twenty-six, I couldn't tell the difference between reality and fantasy. Never to think the fact... whoever owned the house, his or her station in life had to far exceed mine, why would anyone want to explain to me the history, and mystery of a man, who may have killed his wife so many years ago.

I went to splash water on my face and thought about a call to my mother, but knew she'd probably tell me the same thing I'd just told myself. A much needed glass of wine was taken onto the porch, where I sat on the thickly padded wicker rocker, and listened to the sounds of the night... the bay could be heard in the stillness... which surrounded my home.

Tomorrow was Saturday, the shop would open by 9:00 a.m. My thoughts were to finish my glass of wine and go to bed. It would take me sometime to fall asleep. I'd never tell anyone of the humiliation I felt... while trying to be friendly.

Chapter 10

I woke to the sound of engines from the heavy equipment, which may have been leaving the property next door. Even though the adjacent property wasn't close, the loud noise could be heard.

The machinery may have been started most days after I'd leave for the shop. I've never heard it this early. Maybe... whoever the man was last night demanded they start work earlier today, to move the equipment, and begin to straighten out the lawn.

I wouldn't know who *he* was, since he never introduced himself.

Breakfast this morning was put on the back burner... I didn't sleep very well last night... I wasn't hungry and not sure if it was the guy's attitude which bothered me or his exceptionally good looks. Either way, I was tired this morning and looked drained. I'd need cold compresses for my eyes to make me appear wide awake and a touch bit more eyeliner.

My usual daily ritual was to walk to the beach on my property and sit on the stone wall with a cup of coffee. I wouldn't be able to enjoy the early mornings much longer, the fall weather would soon turn cold.

There was a chill in the air. I put on a jacket and set out for my walk hopeful not to see my neighbor. I'd try not to look next door, but straight ahead at the bay.

My walk was slow to the beach. I sat on the wall to gaze at the water... followed it to the horizon... and its vanishing point... think of my existence, and where my place was... in the scheme of life.

The haze, which hung over the bay would soon dissipate as the sun rose higher in the sky. A pair of rubber boots were worn—otherwise my feet would have been wet from the moisture, which appeared as small diamonds, and hugged each individual blade of grass. Once the haze lifted I'd be able to see more of the Bay Bridge... for now it remained a silhouette in the distance.

Born in 1989, by then the Chesapeake Bay Bridge had been completed. It had taken 45 years to connect the eastern and western shores of Maryland. The bridge was 4.35 miles long. The original bridge was opened in 1952. Now there were two spans, north and south bound. I hadn't realized until I'd been back in Claiborne, what a scenic view I'd had in my life.

Being able to view not only the bay with the amazing play of sun and clouds bouncing off the large expanse of water, but with the bridge in its background.

I craved to sit on the lawn of Windward Manor one day, to absorb the capricious view from under the huge trees, which seemed to shade a large section of the gracious mansion.

The sound of the heavy equipment appeared to be upon me and played havoc with my usual tranquil morning and cup of coffee. I couldn't help but look to see what all the noise was about.

It seemed they were ready to backfill and grade the lay of the land. A wall would be built to buffer against the encounter of a severe storm or hurricane, and would not erode, or come close to what would soon be... the newly refurbished manor.

Two figures stood on the recently erected pier. They watched the equipment work its miracle with the dirt. The distance between the two property's didn't allow me a close enough look—to be able to identify either man.

One walked quickly away.

I momentarily realized a man remained on the pier. His stance told me he looked in my direction. A chill ran up and down my spine and remembered my chance meeting last night with the mystery man... my jacket pulled closer, I stood from my seat on the wall, began the walk to my house, and then continued to ready myself for the day... to open the shop.

Today the sun was bright. The heat and its light were needed to shine into my store. The door stood ajar to let in the warmth of the day and remove the chill from the drop in last night's temperature.

The open entry allowed for the many sights and sounds of the busy bay towns regulars and periodic tourists.

Deep in thought I leaned against the doorjamb, absorbing the sun's rays when I heard someone say, "You're the lady next door."

I focused my eyes and realized it was the contractor I'd asked numerous questions of. He held a bag which suggested he'd bought his lunch at Sandwiches and More… since his work began very early this morning.

"Hello… for a Saturday you were at work rather early." I said.

He removed his hat and responded, "Well, my men need to finish up. We promised to have the job on the outside complete by now and a huge lecture was received this morning about why we hadn't finished. I have to say whoever the guy was who chewed me out doesn't have a way with words, and wasn't happy about how the inside work was handled. We're to finish up this week. After today we'll lay sod and hope it takes before the winter sets in." He stopped to shield his eyes from the sun and put his hat back on. "The inside contractor was fired and a new crew will start on Monday, the guy wouldn't listen to the fact the fellas on the inside would move one step forward and two steps back. Someone doesn't like what they intend to change in the house."

I had to ask, "Whoever you spoke with earlier, do you know if he's the owner?"

"I expect so, but he never introduced himself… only raised hell. His beliefs were by now he'd be moved in. But the inside was uninhabitable and he's found his stay at the hotel to be longer. He's not a happy camper." He tipped his hat and said, "Well nice talking with you, got to get back on the job, and done before dark. It was too early to wake the wife to pack me a lunch. I'd heard the sandwich shop was the best around." He paused and nodded, "This your shop?"

"Yes, it was my mother's." I replied. "This was my first summer and I've expanded what we sell. It was a good season with hope it continues a few more weeks, otherwise I may die of boredom."

He gave a chuckle and said, "Nice shop." He provided a wave and left.

After what he'd said, his run in had to be with the same guy who gave me a hard time.

I guess he'll remain anonymous.

Chapter 11

W ith thoughts of the unfriendly neighbor next door, I contemplated the change in my daybreak coffee ritual. In my opinion... I was here first and was not going to let whoever he was... intimidate me. I'd walk, sit or stroll whenever and wherever I wanted ... if it was on my property.

The weather was definitely cooler, but not unbearable... the sun was warm. My early walk to the beach with a jacket and my cup of coffee was how I'd start my day... no one would change it.

Business was great on the weekends, but the weekdays became slow. The shop had done wonderful all season and money was put away. Like my mother said... for *a rainy day*.

Retail being slow the shop would close earlier from Wednesday through Saturday, be closed on Monday's, and Tuesday's. Sunday we opened at10:00 a.m. and closed by 4:00 p.m. This gave me time to enjoy my new friends and begin the indoor renovations on my house.

Alex and Ethan were both handy and since the Crab Shanty's business was at a decline... along with tourism, Ethan found he could earn a few extra dollars by his offer to help me recreate my kitchen from old to modern.

Ava was back in school and Jeanette was in search of a job. We'd shop on Mondays for new and antique items for her home. She was satisfied with the décor of her new house... anyway Ethan said until money grew on trees, she was finished for a while.

Jeanette and I'd shopped for new appliances and cabinets for my kitchen. Except this week. My new kitchen cabinets were to be delivered today. Ethan was to begin to uncrate and set-up until Alex would join him after lunch.

They both had taken time off work and the new kitchen would be ready for the stainless steel appliances by Wednesday. Brittany and Katie would be able to handle the day at the shop. They'd split hours so I'd be available when my appliances arrived.

Excited to see how the new kitchen would look finished, a new floor would be installed, and the room painted. Next would be the bathrooms. Fixtures were on order and when Alex and Ethan were ready I'd have the new pieces delivered.

I couldn't wait.

Thoughts about my neighbor and revelations of how he must have felt since he's had to wait longer for his renovations to be complete before he could move in, bothered me.

I'd noticed when I sat to drink my coffee early yesterday, the outside had come together nicely, from the pool, the apron around the pool, the new sod lawn, the stone wall, and pier... it all turned out spectacular. Even the shrubs the landscapers planted around the pool looked hardy from where I sat. More flowers would be added in the spring... I'm sure... and contractors continued to work on the indoor renovations... I trusted with more luck than they previously had.

I had time for coffee before Ethan and the cabinets arrived and slipped on my jacket to leisurely walk to the wall, sit, and gaze at the bay. The day was sunny and the sun felt great... the temperature would continue to climb throughout the day and fall slightly as the day progressed into night.

I heard chainsaws busy this morning and wondered what was to transpire at Windward Manor. Did I dare take a peek? I'd finish my coffee and walk to the front of my house, which faced the neighbor's property. The oyster shell lane and woods separated our boundaries. Not sure if I'd like, or dislike the new look the manor would take on from the side, and if my privacy would be invaded.

A walk to the front of the property was to see trees fall in the woods around the anterior of the manor house. I thought this was to thin out the wooded area so the smaller trees could continue to grow. The wood would be used to warm the manor through the winter. I watched Ethan drive up the lane and walked towards his car when he got out.

I greeted him and he said, "So what's on the schedule for next door?"

"No idea, Ethan. I liked the wooded area for the seclusion it provided me, but I'm here by myself, maybe it's a good idea to be able to see another house. If only I had the opportunity to speak with someone to find out what was to take place over there, I'd feel better about all of these changes."

"Gosh, remember when I used to ride my bike through those woods?" He asked.

"Yes, and I remember hiding among the trees to watch for my Dad. Mom wouldn't allow me on the side of our house which led to the bay. She forbid me to go anywhere near the water and I couldn't see Dad's boat from the front of our house to know if he was safe, but was glad my bedroom was on the opposite side of the water when the storms came in off the bay. I felt safer."

Before we walked to the house from Ethan's car, the delivery truck with the cabinets arrived. My anticipation was so great, I couldn't contain myself.

I grabbed his arm and yelled, "Ethan, this is better than Christmas."

He smiled and directed the truck.

It was backed to the front porch for easier access to carry the cabinets through the front hall and to the kitchen.

By 1:00 p.m. Alex arrived. Ethan had the cupboards uncrated and ready to hang. I didn't realize it would be so much work. I called for pizza delivery. There was no way for me to make a meal and fit into the kitchen with both men hard at work.

The kitchen looked fabulous and I couldn't believe the difference the new cabinets, counter top, sink, fresh paint, new appliances, and floor made to the older home.

Dinner done. It was still light enough for a walk.

I wanted to stroll along the shore and view the back of Windward Manor out of curiosity, to see if the light in the upper window was lit tonight. Not sure what the status of the new electrical function was and if it had been turned on.

Chapter 12

My last run in with *Mr. Model* of the year, or whatever his name was... remained a mystery and I didn't want to happen into him again. My safest bet was to walk along the shore to see if I could detect the faint light which appeared often in the window.

It was strange to have seen what I thought to be a reflection. It couldn't have been a light since there was no electric in the house the first few times it was apparent... but was it a reflection?

This is what I began to doubt.

I put on my jacket, switched on the outside porch light in case the sun set before my return. This time of year, night seemed to encompass the daylight quickly.

Once near the property line, which divided my domain from Windward Manor's. I walked closer to its pier where I'd felt certain no one would notice me. It wasn't yet twilight and the overall posterior expanse of the house was in full view. I didn't see the light in the upper window and therefore assumed my first reaction... a reflection was probably not the correct theory.

I began my return back home.

Lights, many lights at the same time came on in the manor house.

I froze.

It was as if someone threw one switch and every room in the gracious manor became a glow.

Chills, made my blood run cold. I saw clearly the double set of French doors, which led to the pool area, stood wide-open... they generated a plea to me.

It seemed as though the house wanted to welcome me. Consequently I was drawn to the lights and the open entry. Not able to restrain myself the stone steps between the seawall were ascended.

Automatically I unbolted the black wrought iron gate, which had been put into place when the contractor finished his work on the pier, the wall, and the berm to keep a storm surge at bay.

I walked with resolve at this point and didn't care if anyone was home. Called by an unknown force, there was no way to discourage me. Once the exposed entrance was reached, loudly enough to be heard I yelled, "Hello, is anyone here?"

The wide hallway was entered. I peered into the rooms on either side. They had been renovated to excellence and gave off an appearance it was now 1830. The contractor certainly knew his profession.

The extensive passage was molded out with the widest crown and picture frame details. The mahogany paneled walls, in what was the study or office, were polished to perfection. The broad planked floors were refurbished to a soft luster.

I continued to tread lightly, take in all the new surrounds, and continued to call out. When the central foyer was reached, to glance up the immense stairway was incredible. To gaze upon the portraits along the wall where the stairs rose up to a balcony was stirring.

These had to be the Savage, heads of family. They were three generations of extremely handsome men. To climb the stairs and read the gold nameplates on each portrait was adrenaline-charged for me.

The portrait closest to the bottom of the stairs was Mitchell Thomas Savage, next was Kent Mitchell Savage and the last portrait closes to the top of the stairs was Thomas Mitchell Savage. I'd recognized this name from my research as the first Savage to build and occupy the manor with his wife Elizabeth.

Through my years of study, I'd researched the history and family who'd built and resided in Windward Manor.

Thomas Mitchell Savage and his wife Elizabeth had three children, two sons and a daughter. Their lives at the time were not only considered prosperous, but prestigious.

They used local help, not slaves to maintain their crops. When Thomas and his wife passed, the property was turned over to the youngest son. At the time no one knew exactly why the eldest boy was not considered in the passing down of the home, and ground. But was given a smaller house to reside in—which bordered on their property. After many hours of investigation it was found the oldest son James had a problem with his consumption of alcohol and could not be trusted to the maintenance and care of the estate, its grounds, and the crops.

Kent Mitchell Savage however, was ambitious and the manor and its grounds had flourished until the soil no longer produced hearty crops, due to lack of knowledge on crop rotation. Kent's sister Mary, married and moved to Jamestown, Virginia.

Kent sired five sons with his wife Adeline. From the plantation's earlier profits, Kent and his sons invested in steamboat travel across the Chesapeake Bay. Each was given a parcel of the land to build on, except for the oldest son, Mitchell

Thomas Savage was given Windward Manor as his place to own and reside in.

From the way these men were dressed when the portraits were painted... it was easy to say without the nameplates, the first generation of Savages was at the upper most sector of the stairs. It surprised me to see in all three of the portraits, the gentlemen resembled one another. Their similarity was uncanny.

The man I met here... had to be one of the family members... but his name remained unknown.

On my way down the stairs, I heard a key turn in the front lock and someone shout, "Why, in the hell... are all of the lights on?"

Before I could take the last few stairs, run down the long hall, and out through the open French doors... I gazed intently into those bluer than blue eyes with an icy stare. He began to yell so violently I covered my ears.

The lights began to flicker and dim. They flashed and dimmed to the point of darkness, he softened his tone, stood with his hands on his hips and said, "What's going on here?"

I explained what happened. How all the lights came on at once, the doors were open, and how I'd been drawn to the house.

Meekly I said, "I asked if anyone was home before I entered and wanted to make sure no one was hurt or in need of help."

He finally spoke slowly and adversely after he listened to my explanation and said, "There is no way all of these lights would have come on at the same time. I only left one small fixture lit... to see when I came back tonight with my clothing."

When this was said, every light except for the one he left on went out.

I gasped, "I don't know your name, but gather from the portraits you have to be related to the Savage family, but how and who you are... has me frightened? I think there is someone in this house other than the two of us."

At this all of the lights came on again.

He looked at me, but this time his eyes softened and he said, "I'm the 5th generation of Savages'. My father was the 4th, but never occupied this house or wanted anything to do with it... my grandmother passed it on to me. I'm named after the second generation... Kent Mitchell Savage, but acknowledged as Mitch Savage... and I'm sorry... but I've seemed to have forgotten your name."

I was shaken from the force I felt in this house. It wasn't a bad force, but scary all the same. His mockery about the forgotten name infuriated me to the point of answering him in the similar manor. Shoulders squared, hand extended and with a bit of contempt came the reply, "Kristen Kendal... your neighbor."

His eyes revealed his distain, but accepted my hand. Whatever energy was in the house... locked his with mine. I was conscious of his touch in my heart. He recognized it too... but preferred not to acknowledge the awareness. At this the lights went out... except for the minor light in the foyer... until Mitch switched on the foyer's chandelier.

He didn't seem one bit shaken by the ghostly experience.

Chapter 13

My association with Mitch wasn't in the least bit pleasant. He listened to the reason I'd entered his home and stated he'd begin to move his possessions into the section of the house where work had been completed. It was indicated to be a warning.

He'd made the comment about the lights and how the electrician must have crossed wires... because he didn't believe in ghosts or spirits.

All I could say was good for him... because there was an influence in this house I recognized... not a bad one necessarily... but it was quite apparent.

He abruptly said goodnight to dismiss me and sent me out... through the front door.

Every light outside and in the house went on again. I was pleased, because it allowed enough brilliance for me to reach my home and not be engulfed in total darkness.

My outside entry light was lit and gave me the luminosity needed to enter by the side screened in porch.

I locked the wood framed screen door... which was certainly of no protection, entered into my newly renovated kitchen, closed, and locked the kitchen door. The windows and entrances on the first level were secured.

With beliefs about what had taken place next door and the low illumination in the hall on the second floor of my home —I peered through the center front dormered upstairs window.

There I knelt on the cushioned window seat to collect my emotions and gaze through the residual trees to see if the lights in Windward Manor had turned themselves off.

The house from the side seemed dark, except for its lone window—where a very soft glow of light remained. It resembled the identical light a candle may disclose. It was the same light visible each night I'd walk along the shoreline... sure now... beyond all certainty... it was not a reflection.

I wished to know which room the light existed and who may have occupied it—before the house had been boarded up. It appeared to be the only window on the second floor, on this side of the entire manor, which happened to look upon my residence. I wondered if whatever spirit was in the manor... watched my home years before the mansion was shuttered... or since the boards had been removed.

The best way to find out about the light and room was to inspect the county records and see if there were blue prints or diagrams on the plans of Windward Manor.

I'd ask Ethan tomorrow if the chronicles would show evidence or a layout of the house... and what department I'd need to check with.

I sat and gazed at the faint light and tried to reason with myself about my obsession with the manor and the magnetism I felt towards Mitch.

He attracted me like no other man— not even Corbin.

There was something about Mitch which appeared to make him forbidden, like drinking alcohol during prohibition.

His mood could be gloomy like an overcast day, and my thoughts were riddled with the discovery of his deepest secrets. I prayed he could hear the beating whispers from my heart.

Before I left the window seat to go to my room, I turned off the light in the hall, but continued to wonder why the glow was still apparent in the manor's window.

My sleep became restless. Was it a dream? A vision of blue, ice blue eyes which held an abundant of mystery for me, but also a love, so safe, secure, and protected from the same eyes which held mine... in a silent look of love.

My nightmare became intense. I wandered through the manor up to the room which glowed in the nightfall's darkness, sensed eyes on me bluer than the sky, and turned to see Mitch in a slow walk behind me. I stopped. He caught up to me and took my hand. It was taken in affection. I reached out to turn the knob on the bedroom door... and woke in a sweat. It seemed real. I had to have been there before—maybe in another time?

I left my bedroom and went to sit on the window seat to see if the candle glow of light could be seen in the mansions window. It was1:00 a.m. and the glimmer was gone. I needed to sleep and shake the sensation from my dream... the manor... and Mitch.

What was it about Kristen Kendal. I haven't been able to halt my thoughts on the raven haired beauty, with the smoky—steely—gray eyes. I've never seen eyes the color of hers. I've heard about, but never seen this shade. They held kindness and a gentleness which appealed to some sense of respect I didn't know existed in me.

After the stories my grandmother told about love and life, I wasn't sure I'd want anything to do with a wife. A mistress perhaps, but no one permanently.

My father wasn't the greatest father or husband in the world and from what my grandmother expressed to me, neither was my grandfather. Grandmother would say, the Savage men were cursed with the noble looks of being extraordinarily attractive, but they needed a heart. I remember her saying she raised me with love, tenderness, and expected me to show more civility, chivalry, and love to a woman... more than the last two generations of Savage men.

I've possibly started off on the wrong foot with Kristen. There was a need to be cautious not to scare her completely away before I knew what her mysteries held for me. Once I'd taste her mouth, I'd be lost to her forever. This torment about her needed to stop so I could obtain a goodnights sleep.

Chapter 14

W ell I certainly hadn't had an abundance of sleep. The dreams continued till dawn. Each one was different, but Mitch was in them all. Today would be the day to investigate and find the layout, or blueprints on the manor.

Ethan was called and asked if he knew where I could locate the information needed. He gave me the name and number of the gentleman he'd used to obtain his building permits for the expansion of his deck. His thoughts were Richard Worth would be able to help me.

A call was made.

I headed to the recorder of deeds and permits for Claiborne. It was off the main highway, in a new office building. It retained many of the small bay front communities' permits and deeds.

When I gave my name at the front counter Mr. Worth stepped from behind his desk. Introduced his self and made me aware it was against policy to give out information if it did not pertain to my home.

He looked over his bifocals and said, "The building permit for the renovations on Windward Manor does show a blue print, but I'm not allowed to share it with you."

I was disappointed, but it was senseless to tell him about the soft glow of light, which was seen at night, or how all the lights came on, and went off at the same time.

He must have read my disappointment, "Ms. Kendal, I'm sorry, but I'm sure once your neighbor meets you, he'll be glad to give you a tour of his lovely home."

"Mr. Worth, I wouldn't be too sure of this. But the house holds a certain mystery for me and I wanted to know what the back room in the upper corner of the house may have been used for?"

He winked at me and pressed keys on the computer, looked at the screen for a few moments and then said, "Years ago the room you're inquisitive about was considered a sitting room off a bedroom. It's all I can tell you."

I thanked him and left the office. This wasn't much help. But I now knew... more than before. Who was up there and why did they watch my house? What was in this particular room... and what happened years ago to perpetuate the glimmer of soft light?

The days passed quickly towards colder weather. I'd not seen Mitch anywhere in town. But knew he was at Windward Manor. Lights could be seen when I went on my early evening stroll. They had to come from the study and kitchen. I was definitely aware of those two rooms and their location, when the doors stood open and lights drew me inside.

After my twilight walk and return home, I was unable to see if other luminosities were lit in the manor except for the one in the upper corner of the house which faced mine.

All seemed quiet.

I occupied my slow time at work by having the bathrooms in my house refurbished and it finally became a home.

Jeanette and I shopped, but for me this time. My home needed new accessories. I'd found many and dishes to fit with my newly renovated kitchen.

The shop, which was now practically closed except for weekends, was locked early enough to gather with my friends at the Crab Shanty, enjoy the crabs from the Carolinas, and the oysters from the Chesapeake Bay, which made the best fried oyster sandwiches and stew.

One problem with this time of year on the bay… were the storms which rolled in. I'd been to the Crab Shanty earlier, my usual Sunday evening, and was now home ahead of the rainstorm the weather analysts had predicted.

The forecast reported heavy rain, high winds and coastal flooding. There wasn't a moon, or star in the sky, and the bay churned. The white caps splashed off the seawall.

This was the only drawback of living on my own.

Alex and Ava asked if I wanted to stay with them… but I had to become used to an encounter of this type of storm. I didn't mind a typical thunderstorm… well I did… but I could handle them.

This storms forecast was for high winds, thunder and lightning to ground strikes. I was glad the house had lightning rods or it could have been far scarier for me.

My home had a center hallway, which wasn't very long, but wide enough to be cozy. I'd hide myself between the large country kitchen and living room on a queen size air mattress, which if I had to… could be slept on through the night.

The porch on the front of the house was some protection from the wind to the front, but the winds would come from the side which accommodated the screened in porch.

The canvas roll-down, sunshades were secured at the top of the screen for air flow. The back of the house had the laundry room and half bath. There was no way I would sleep upstairs tonight.

Pillows, blankets, batteries, a few flashlights, candles, matches, a good book, snacks, and drinks surrounded me. This is where I intended to stay hunkered down until the storm passed.

Of course I had my cell phone and laptop. So far the electric was on. The living room being the furthest from the winds had too many windows to be safe from the lightning.

The hard downpour of rain could be heard. It battered the tin roof on the second floor of the house. The lighting and thunder were almost synonymous with one another, the thunderstorm was on top of us. The wind howled and I heard its eerie sound as it whistled through the screened in porch.

The crashing sounds heard had to be the synchronized lighting and thunder, but could have been trees in the wooded area hit by lightning then toppled upon the ground.

Glad I'd moved the car into the area along the living room side of the house. The space provided some protection from the trees and wind.

My laptop was in use when the electric went out. The battery was fully charged and would last a few hours, and then I'd read until I became sleepy.

I needed to use the small bathroom at the end of the hall and hurry back to my secure place hidden from the storm.

I'd barely settled myself on the air mattress… when a significant bang on my front door was heard. I became alarmed.

This wasn't the time to open the door to a stranger—while alone.

The loud knock stopped. My name was called at full volume, "Kristen... Kristen, it's Mitch." Then the sudden noise began again. I headed towards the door.

I tried to yell back over the wind, thunder, and lightning strikes, "Okay, Mitch. Give me a second."

The front door was opened and I tried my best to keep it from being blown into the wall. Mitch, awkwardly stomped into my house. There was blood... and it poured from a gash on his forehead. He was soaked through and looked pale... even in the faint light.

Shocked to see him in such a state I asked, "Mitch... what happened? Sit down. Let me grab a towel for your head."

I grabbed one of the blankets and wrapped it around his shoulders. He was cold, his lips appeared blue... but tempting.

What was wrong with me... why would I have thoughts about his mouth at a time like this?

I ran to the bathroom, grabbed a few more towels. He was seated on the air mattress with his back against the wall with an expression of pure numbness. I knelt next to him, wiped away the wetness from the rain and the blood—to see how badly he was injured.

The snacks, drinks and other items were pushed out of the way to move around him. I asked again, "What happened?"

He concentrated, it seemed he couldn't form the words, but then began to speak.

"I knew the storm would be wicked... I went out to re-park my car, moved it from under the trees, was headed back to the house when a large branch fell, knocked me down, and I think out." He paused and touched his head. "When I finally got up and reached the house... the door was locked. Don't ask me how, I didn't lock it, and then I couldn't find my keys. They flew out of my hand when the branch hit me. I'm sorry, but there was nowhere else to go. I may need a few stitches." He expressed with apology.

I gently applied pressure to the gash in his head, "You're right about the stitches, but not tonight. I'll try to butterfly the cut and hope it slows the flow of blood. Let me grab ice from the kitchen, then I'll bandage your head. Can I get you anything else?"

He looked around at my survival goods and gave me a beautiful smile, which stunned me, "I think you have everything you need right here." He whispered.

He was right… and my eyes were on him.

Chapter 15

A dry blanket or two was needed from upstairs. With the light from my flashlight, the wound was cleaned and butterflied, which was larger than previously anticipated. Mitch's head was wrapped with gauze. He needed to get out of his wet shirt and pants.

The best I could do was to give him a blanket to wrap around himself to keep warm. A beach towel and a few large safety pins would have to work as a kilt for the lower half of his body. His color was back in his lips when I gave him three Tylenol for his headache.

He made his way to the half bath with a flashlight to remove his wet garments. Without electric his clothes could not be dried. The kilt was now in place from his waist down.

To gaze upon him, was magnificent. His broad shoulders, muscled arms, rippled chest and abs made my heart pound. His blue eyes said thank you and so did he. My thoughts were for what? I should thank him for his company. When a girl has the pleasure to look upon such a wonderful specimen she should be thankful... and I was.

The storm wasn't near its end, as a matter of fact it sounded worse. I'm glad someone was with me.

My cell phone rang. I answered. A finger was placed in my one ear to hear over the force of the storm.

"Hello?"

"Kristen, are you okay?" I could sense Ethan's concern.

"I'm fine, Ethan. You remember how we used to camp out when we were kids and it stormed."

"Yes, the downstairs hallway."

"Well it's where I am… in the hallway. I'm prepared for a change and have company."

"Company… who in their right mind would be out in this weather?"

"My neighbor was locked out. A tree limb had fallen on him. He was lucky to make it here in one piece."

"You okay with this, Kristen?" He inquired.

"I'm good, Ethan. Thanks for checking on me. How's Cory, did she adjust to the storm?" I asked.

He replied, "She actually fell asleep between Jeanette and me in our bed. I'll check with you tomorrow, if you need me call."

"Thanks, Ethan." I said.

I saw a smile creep onto Mitch's face, "Boyfriend… checking on you?"

"No, a childhood friend… married with a child. When we were kids, we used to make a fort in this hallway when it stormed. My mom always said it was the safest place in the house."

"I can tell you… it's cozy here." Mitch paused and took in the area, "I can't imagine a hideout anywhere in my huge house. Maybe I was locked out on purpose, by the spirit you think is harbored in the manor." He began to laugh.

"Mitch, it's not funny. Now is not a good time to talk about it, but we will. For now I'd like to know where you're from, what you do for a living… are you hungry?"

Now I laughed when I saw his expression. Too many questions at once.

He stated, "I did miss dinner tonight and didn't get back to the house early enough to fix supper before the storm rolled in. I watched it come off the bay. I've never seen anything so evil in my life. I've never lived this close to the water before. I'll take the storm warnings seriously next time, and be prepared... or I can come over here with you." He winked.

"You know, Mitch... I do like the company. I've never lived here by myself before and I can say—this is one hell of a storm and I'm scared. What would you like to eat? A ham sandwich or tuna. I have potato salad."

"The ham sandwich sounds good. I'm not sure if I feel queasy from lack of food, or from the hit on the head, and appreciate your help. I realize... I haven't been the most pleasant neighbor."

I smiled, "It's okay, but it will cost you. I want you to tell me about yourself... and your family. Mayo or mustard, cheese... lettuce?"

"If it's going to cost me—I'll take the works." He said.

Into the kitchen we went. He followed with the flashlight, but should have been seated after being knocked out. I felt safer from the storm with him. He stood close by and asked what he could do.

"I'll get the bread... you can grab a soda. I'll take care of the rest." I responded.

It was late and I was hungry myself... from all of the excitement of the storm, to Mitch... here with me.

A tray was taken from the pantry, two plates from the cupboard, two sandwiches made and potato salad scooped onto each one. The silverware drawer was opened and two forks removed.

A few times while the storm's fury continued I'd jump and couldn't wait to move back into the safety of the hall. I carried the tray. We sat with pillows behind our backs on the air mattress. Mitch was handed a plate... I grabbed mine, and sat the tray aside.

My body jumped in fear, at the lighting strikes, and thunder.

Chapter 16

To try and take my mind off the fear I felt, Mitch began his story of where he grew up, lived with his parents the first few years of his life, and then why they divorced.

"My mother moved out west and I haven't seen or heard from her in years. My Dad passed in a work related accident."

I felt sorry for him and my heart wept.

"My grandmother was my lifeline." He said. "She had a strong constitution and stories were told to me about my grandfather, his callousness and unemotional attachment to her and her needs. She was brought to Windward Manor as a young girl of sixteen, a servant to my grandfather." He took another bite of his sandwich and a drink. "I was told after a short time she became more than his servant. When she found she was pregnant, they were married in Virginia. She wasn't happy and thought it best to leave." He paused as I watched his reaction to this sad story. "Grandmother took the marriage license with her and left the house at night as a stowaway on a boat to Virginia and later made her way to New York. They were never divorced... my grandfather never filed for one."

I had to speak up, "I don't know if you realize this, but the history books and the town believe he may have killed her or she drowned in the bay and her body never found."

"Yes. My grandmother told me of the rumors. But she let

my grandfather know where she was. He never came after her. He died and the house became boarded up, it was placed in an estate to be divided among relatives. When my grandmother heard of his death, she came forward with the marriage license, and my father's birth certificate. It's taken time to prove I'm the next legal generation of Savages'. My grandmother was given an allotment for years from my grandfather for support. This had all been done through his lawyer, which could be the reason why no one knew what happened to her."

I was almost finished with my sandwich... but Mitch talked so much a small portion of his remained.

He continued to say, his grandmother taught him to be kind, gentle, thoughtful and generous.

I had to laugh at him. "Mitch, I can only ask... what happened?" It was said with sarcasm.

He did grin when he said, "Kristen... at the time of our first encounter I had business problems, then the contractors told me the house was haunted. Work wasn't finished... I was tired of life from a suitcase and then... there... was you."

I wasn't sure if this was meant to be good or indifferent.

"Timing couldn't have been worse. I'm sorry. I know it doesn't make up for the two times I was inconsiderate, tactless for that matter. I knew better, but all I was interested in was to get settled, bring my grandmother back home... although she insists she doesn't want to live here, and wants to remain in New York."

"You know, Mitch, I've told you before... there's a mystery which surrounds the woman and what happened to her. It's documented in the history of the manor."

He was serious and so were those blue eyes which held me captive, "I know. I've heard about and read the mystery of

Windward Manor. My grandmother told me to be careful, but like I said—I don't believe in ghosts or spirits."

I was tired and didn't want to get into what my thoughts were on the manor. Empty dishes were placed on the tray and carried to the kitchen. There was the loudest crash. I screamed. Mitch came to take hold of me.

"Holy mackerel." Mitch said. "That was the closest hit yet. It sounded like it crashed in the trees. Is there a way to see from the upstairs window to my place?"

"Yes. Follow me." I carried two flashlights, one lit and the other in case this one died.

We went up the center stairway to the window seat. It was hard to see what happened until the next brilliant crack of lightning shot through the sky. One large tree had been hit and laid across the oyster shell lane. I concentrated so hard on the tree which was downed and thankful I'd moved my car... I hadn't looked elsewhere.

Mitch whispered, "Kristen, is there a light in the window?"

I turned to face him. His eyes implored me, "Mitch... it's one of the things I've wanted to ask you about. There is always a soft glow of light apparent in the side window. I saw it first from the back of the house and when you thinned out the trees... it's seen from here. It usually goes off late, but is seen each night. My first thoughts were it was a reflection when the sunset and the moon began its rise, but it's not. There is no explanation for it. It's like the night all the lights went on at the same time and drew me inside your home."

I sensed the disbelief in his voice, "We haven't started to work in this wing of the house. Maybe someone was up there and left a light lit."

"Mitch, face it. This light was apparent when there wasn't

electric in the house and who would turn it off and on. There is an unsettled spirit in the manor. I don't feel it's dangerous but…"

"But the bastard locked me out of my home in this damn storm."

I smiled and said demurely, "He may have had a reason."

He looked at me from the glow of the flashlight, "What in the hell kind of reason could he have?" He beseeched me with a certain anger in his voice.

"I don't know Mitch?" Maybe it was for us to become friends, maybe more. After the dreams I'd had who knows. His grandmother and I needed to eventually talk.

Back to the safety of the hallway we conversed for a while longer, I began to yawn, and the storm continued in full force. Occasionally fire sirens were heard. Mitch wasn't able to go anywhere. The darkness outside was only bright intermittently when the lightning flashed. He'd never find his keys until morning light. We continued to put ice on the gash in his head. It would soon be time for more Tylenol. We both needed sleep.

The snacks and goodies were pushed aside, we moved our pillows, and placed them at the head of the air mattress. We'd been seated with our backs against the wall and each had a blanket to cover with, keep us warm, and it seemed less intimate this way.

Chapter 17

My alarm was set to give Mitch another dose of Tylenol. He'd been awake long enough and would be safe for him to sleep. I'd checked head injury and knocked unconscious on my iPhone. It said to wake him often. There were only so many hours left in the night.

I'd do my best.

The alarm was to go off every hour for the next four hours, to wake Mitch.

An hour passed. He was to be given more Tylenol and was gently nudged.

He expressed in a low murmur, "I'm sorry to be a pain, Kristen, but my head hurts."

"I don't know what else to do for you. The ice pack is warm, let me see if I have another one." I whispered with sympathy.

He sounded defeated, "No. It's okay... it hurts when the cold touches my head."

Enough with the ice I thought.

"Mitch, the bleeding has stopped. I'll have to take you to the hospital first thing tomorrow. Try to go back to sleep. I'm sorry, but I'll have to wake you in an hour."

He seemed harder to wake the second time, but I found we were nestled in a spoon position with his arm across me. It seemed so natural and felt better than right. When I woke him all I needed to do was ask him his name and let him go back to sleep.

This continued until I fell into a sound sleep. The dreams were about the manor, Mitch, and me... they appeared to be real.

I woke with a start. It was quiet, and the sun was bright.

Quietly I said, "Mitch... Mitch, wake up. The storm has passed. It's..." my iPhone was scanned, "Its 10:00 o'clock."

His arm still around me... he responded slowly and had a hard time opening those baby blues. Once he looked at me... I saw his pupils were dilated.

"Mitch, how do you feel?" I asked.

"I've felt better. Can't seem to focus well today. I feel nauseated." He said in a groggy voice.

"The electric isn't on. There's no way to dry your clothes. I can't take you to the hospital for stitches in what you're now covered in. Do you feel well enough for me to take you home... look for the keys, dress, and then we'll leave for the hospital? If you weren't in need of stitches... I'd put you upstairs to rest in the guest room."

He began to unwrap himself from me, and said, "Maybe a cup of coffee is what I need and I'll feel better."

I stood up to put on coffee. "Lie still until I put on clean clothes, then I'll start the coffee."

He did as suggested.

First I went into the kitchen and looked out the window. Even though the storm had subsided the bay nevertheless was rough, but ebbed. It appeared the seawall held back the water.

Once upstairs I peered out the center window and saw the destruction of trees in the woods between our houses... and changed quickly. Washed my face. Ran a brush through my hair, brushed my teeth, and returned downstairs.

Mitch laid still, with his hand across the uninjured portion of his forehead. I stepped lightly on the air mattress not to jostle him, went to the kitchen to make coffee... and realized there was no way without the coffee maker... the electric was off, tea was all I had to offer since the gas stove remained on.

I handed him the tea, "Mitch, with the electric off I can't make coffee."

He sat up to taste the tea, only took a sip, and sat in a dazed state.

"Mitch..." He looked at me, my heart skipped a beat. He was the sexiest man I'd ever seen, even with his head wrapped in gauze. "I need to get you home. Then to the hospital. Do you think you can walk to the car?"

"I hope so." He replied.

He didn't seem very talkative and appeared pale.

"Would you rather stay here and tell me where your clothes are? I'll bring them back, so you can change." I stated.

The look he gave me was one of concern when he asked, "Can you ... please? If you find the keys, open the trunk of the car... there's a gym bag and a clean set of clothes. I don't want you to go into the house by yourself."

I nodded my head in a positive manner and said, "Rest, Mitch. I'll be back soon."

He laid back down.

"I'll walk through the woods, it will be faster." I exclaimed.

He rolled onto his side and leaned up on his elbow, "Kristen, drive. Trees may be ready to fall or limbs could break and drop. You could be injured."

Okay I guess he could be right. I grabbed the keys and went to my car. The tree which fell last night dropped perfectly and left me enough room to maneuver my vehicle out of its spot and onto the shell lane.

I drove with speed and approached the manor. Trees were down. Others leaned against one another. One strong breeze and they'd fall like pick-up sticks.

It was a mess. The huge limb close to the front door had to be the one to hit Mitch. Its diameter was at least seven inches. No wonder his head hurt. It took me a few minutes to locate the keys. They were wet and muddy. I'd have to open the truck with the key and not the fob. The gym bag was in plain sight, removed from the trunk, and back to my house I went.

Mitch was asleep. I had to wake him, he needed to see a doctor. I touched his shoulder gently and softly said, "I'm back... and have your clothes."

He appeared confused, he sat up, and was handed his things.

"Can you turn around until I pull on my briefs? Will you help me dress? I'm sure you have seen men in less." He asked.

I laughed, "I have."

"So you're okay with this?" He looked and sounded uneasy.

"Yes, Mitch... let me assist you." I said.

It was cold outside. I wrapped the blanket around his shoulders and helped him to the car. He didn't have a coat. When he came last night all he wore was a dress shirt and pants, his coat must have been in the house.

I saw him tremble, turned the heat, and heated seat on.

Medical attention wasn't far. The decision was made to take him to Urgent Care. He needed immediate attention. The almost five miles across the Bay Bridge was too far to travel. When we arrived at the emergency facility, I parked in the pick-up and drop-off zone, went in, and asked for a wheel chair. A doctor followed to help with Mitch.

I sat in the waiting room while he was examined. Eventually they called me back to his cubical and told he had a concussion, and shouldn't be left alone.

He'd need to be looked after and required rest. There were ten stitches and seemed to be a lot of staples. Stitches in his forehead and staples in his scalp. They shaved a section of his hair, but it didn't take away from his handsome face.

The nurse handed me an antibiotic ointment to apply to the damaged area, along with medication to help for headaches, and an antibiotic. They helped me put him in the car and we left for home. I wasn't sure which home at the moment… I needed to ask.

"Mitch, you have two choices, one is to stay with me, and the other is for me to stay at the manor with you."

He looked perceptively at me, "Kristen, until I can further investigate what if anything is apparent at Windward Manor… I don't want you there. Do you mind if I stay with you. I promise not to be too much of a bother."

"You're in luck." I said. "My shop is closed during the week and I'm available to play nurse." I reached my hand across the seat and gently laid it on his arm. "Mitch, I'm sorry you've been hurt … I know it's hard for you to ask for my help, but I don't mind at all."

He touched my hand with his and melted me with those blue eyes which no longer appeared… as cold as ice.

Chapter 18

W e'd returned home. I'd make him comfortable upstairs in the spare bedroom. It was freshly painted in a neutral shade, and ready for a guest. I was ecstatic the visitor... was Mitch.

Most of the time I fantasized about him and here he was to stay for at least the week.

He was settled. I needed to make us both a meal. The electric was back on. I had homemade vegetable soup in the freezer, thawed it in the microwave, and then was placed in a pot to slowly heat. We'd have slices of French bread... buttered, sliced apple, and sharp cheese to add to the brunch meal. We missed breakfast and it was too early for lunch.

My cell phone rang. I was about to carry the food upstairs. It was Ethan. The tray rest on the counter in order for me to answer the phone.

"Hello, Ethan. Did everyone make it through the storm? I heard the fire alarm a few times last night. It was noisy from the storm, but the sirens could be heard. Was anyone hurt?" I inquired.

"No one battered and yes we're okay, everyone made it. A few fires, but nothing major, no injuries. I wanted to check on you. Still have company?" He asked.

"I do, and he'll be here for the week or until he feels better.

He has a nasty cut on his head and a concussion. There's a big tree down across my lane and many more in the woods. It's a mess over here. If you need firewood, bring a saw."

"Kris, are you sure you're okay with him for the week?"

"Sure, why not… he needs help. I'm off until the weekend. We'll be okay, but you can always stop by to check if it makes you feel better." I giggled.

I heard him respond to my laugh, "No." Before he said, "Then again maybe I will. You need anything from the store? How about I take a look at the tree?"

"We'll be here and no we're good on food. Catch you later." I hit end on the phone and laughed to myself. Ethan my protector.

The tray was picked up once again and carried upstairs. I hoped Mitch's soup wasn't cold by now.

There was a nightstand next to the bed. I placed the tray part of the way onto it to move the light and make room for the entire platter. Mitch was asleep on his back. I hated to wake him, but I needed to… he had to eat.

I spoke softly, "Mitch…" He opened his eyes and turned towards me. My heart seemed to race each time I looked at him. Those eyes and his striking features stirred me.

"I brought you brunch. You need to eat."

He tried to sit up. I pulled the pillow up behind his back. He leaned against it and said, "Thanks. What smells so good?"

"Soup, but there's bread, sliced apple, and cheese. It should be enough to hold you over for a while."

I put the legs down on the tray and placed it over his lap. I needed to go back to the kitchen for his drink. I'd have my soup downstairs.

"Kristen, will you eat?" He inquired.

"Yes, I'll get your drink and eat downstairs."

He grabbed my hand gently. "Can you eat here with me? I could use the company. Plus we need to talk."

I shook my head okay and said, "Alright, I'll be back."

He was right we did need to talk. I wanted to know what was going on in that house of his. My thoughts were his grandmother may know more than what she'd told him.

This may be two trips upstairs unless I can figure out how to get two drinks and a bowl of soup upstairs without a mess. Ice in a freezer baggie, two plastic cups, napkins, and two cans of soda in a plastic grocery bag would work. I placed my hand through the handles and moved it up my arm and carried my reheated bowl of soup upstairs... after I managed to get through the maze in my hallway.

I'd need to clear my hall of the air mattress and other emergency paraphernalia.

Upstairs my bowl was sat on Mitch's tray until the plastic bag on my arm, was unloaded, drinks prepared, and the chair pulled close to the bed. We were now ready to eat and talk.

"I have a few questions of my own." I informed him.

Chapter 19

M itch ate slowly. He appeared to be in pain. "You look like you're ready for your next dose of pain medication."

"I'd say. It even hurts to chew. Thanks for the soup... good choice. I'll pass on the bread for now. The meds make me sleepy... I want to talk first. I don't know much about you. Can you tell me about yourself? How you ended up in this house? It was once part of Windward Manor... in its prime."

I was aware of this.

I took the time to talk about my family. How I acquired the house and how long I'd lived here before my move to San Francisco. We talked about my engagement and break-up, my move back home, the shop, but most importantly my obsession with Windward Manor's history... and the manor house itself.

Before Mitch could reply, there was an outrageous knock on my front door. I stood up from the chair. Mitch grabbed my arm. Ours eyes locked. I sensed his deep concern. He'd be up here and I'd be downstairs... possibly to open the door to trouble.

The loud obnoxious noise continued, "Kristen... look first... be careful. I don't like the sound of that knock." Mitch warned.

"I'll be okay. We've never had any problems around here." I stated with the confidence I was right.

He let go of my arm gradually, until he gently captured my hand and held it for a brief second. My thoughts went immediately to his touch... which set my heart to flutter like the wings of a butterfly. I had to turn my head to escape the look in his blue eyes, they held me captive and so did he.

Down the stairs I ran, the loud troubled bang continued, it felt safer to look through the door's peep hole first... and couldn't believe what I saw.

I opened the door suddenly and stated with authority, "What is wrong with you? A continuous noise like this could wake the dead. I'm not deaf and besides... why are you here?" It was said with animosity.

He was loud and yelled at me, "What the hell were you trying to prove when I was here weeks ago. The guy who said he was engaged to you is married, it was all a bullshit line. Why couldn't we have a decent conversation without his interference... friend or not." He paused to catch his breath. "I asked around—Ethan, I think is his name, followed you to San Francisco, he came back here, went in the service, is now married, and I assume still a good friend, because this is how small towns work—but it doesn't give him or you the right to lie about it."

I was vindictive, "My, my, from the number one liar himself. You have a lot of nerve, Corbin."

I heard the loud conversation. Decided I needed to get myself out of bed, see what the problem was, and who would have the nerve to scream at Kristen. The guy had to be crazy and she yelled back. What the h…?

"Kristen, are you okay?" I yelled from the top of the stairs. I turned to see Mitch. He made his way down a few stairs. "Mitch, you shouldn't be out of bed. Please be careful, you're not steady on your feet… you could fall."

"I'm okay, what's …?"

Mitch became quiet. It was said in an unbelievable tone, "Corbin… why are you here?"

I was bewildered and looked from one to the other… "You two know one another?" I inquired.

Mitch answered first, "He works for my company. Handles San Francisco. The company office is based out of New York."

I watched Mitch sit down on one of the steps, his appearance was disturbingly pale.

"Mitch, are you alright? Your color isn't good. Don't pass out on me. Let me help you back to bed." I said.

"No… I want to hear what Corbin has to say. I don't appreciate the tone he's used with you. What's going on, please explain why you're here? It sounds as though you and Kristen were in a relationship… which is over?"

The change in Corbin's manor became evident. "Look, Mitch, this isn't business. It has nothing to do with you. I came to straighten out a few mix-ups Kristen and I've had. We'd been engaged a number of years… she broke off the engagement, came back here, gave up her home, her job, me… and I want to know why?"

I hugged myself and laughed. "Oh my God, Corbin… how can you stand there and deny any wrong doing? I found you cheated on me and if you think that doesn't constitute the end to an engagement, than you seriously try to kid yourself about how stupid you really think I am."

"You never let me explain." He expressed.

It was my turn to be irritated, "Corbin, there was no explanation needed. I don't care if she blindfolded you and attacked you... you've had numerous affairs since we'd been engaged."

The door was open. I saw through the glass storm door, Ethan and Alex drive up in Ethan's truck. He came to the door and heard me scream at Corbin and opened the storm door.

I looked at him and said, "Don't say a word."

His hands shot up in the air and said, "That's a big tree lying across your lane."

I began to laugh, and said, "Thanks, Ethan... I needed a good laugh, but what I don't need is this man who's attempted to weasel out of an affair or two or three to tell me I won't let him explain. Sorry Corbin, but you have got to go... end of story."

He wasn't ready to give up, "Tell me how does one woman have four men at her house... at the same time and claim innocence?"

I placed my hands on my hips, "They are all welcome here, but you can leave." I pointed at the door. Corbin looked surprised at my command. "And... Mitch, you need to get back upstairs in bed, Ethan and Alex if you have your saws, please get started on the tree. That's all I'm going to say... thank you gentlemen."

I turned to help Mitch upstairs... his hand came up, "Wait." He said... "I have a question for Corbin. If you've been engaged to this beautiful woman for years, then why... when we had company functions... haven't I met her?"

I saw him raise his eyebrows. I'm sure Mitch had been introduced to many women over the past few years, because Corbin wouldn't think to go to an event without a date... and he certainly never asked me.

A fire stirred in Corbin's eyes, "What the hell are you doing in her house, Mitch, and her bedroom for that matter? Is she the same nosy neighbor you spoke about the other week?"

I voiced, "He's not in my bedroom… but in the guest room. He was injured in the storm and it's none of your business who I invite into my home. Please go away."

Corbin finally left with a revengeful attitude. I heard the chainsaws and knew Ethan and Alex began to cut up the tree.

I viewed Mitch with query. "Can this nosy neighbor—help you back to bed?"

A hold was taken on his arm to help him. Corbin's remark upset me, plus his nerve to actually show up at my house. Finally up the steps and in the guest room, I gazed into Mitch's blue eyes, and assisted him in his quest to sit on the bed.

"Is this how you think of me?" I asked softly.

He smiled and whispered, "You know I apologized once, already."

I responded less timidly, "Yes you did. And thank you for what you said to Corbin." Distressed, I asked quietly and turned my back to him not to expose tears I felt begin to take formation, "How many different women did he bring to those affairs your company sponsored?"

Did I really want to know? The first time I learned of his unfaithfulness was offensive enough and now to learn this… was way past devastation for me.

Mitch touched my hand and gently forced me to turn and gaze at him. The look on his face said he read my anguish. His answer couldn't have been more perfect when he said, "None… as beautiful as you."

It was said with pure sincerity.

Chapter 20

I helped Mitch lie back against the pillows. He didn't appear well. I sensed he was in pain and handed him his drink, he took hold of it. When he had a firm grip, the pain medication was placed in his other hand.

He took it and said, "When I wake up... can we talk?"

Of course I said, "Yes, because I want to know what your business is about. I'm aware Corbin works for an international container shipment corporation. I'm not exactly sure what he does. I'm familiar with the fact he travels often to the East Coast. I've suspected he cheated on me all along." I sighed and fixed the blankets for him, "Get some rest... if you can with the noise outside. Maybe the guys can come back tomorrow?"

He raised his hand in a simple gesture to stop me. "No. I'll be okay. Let them get the tree out of the way. I'll pay them if they want to take care of the fallen trees on my property."

"I'll ask. I'm sure Ethan will be happy to assist you. He needs work this time of year. His business is slow right now. Rest easy, Mitch. When you wake I'll have dinner ready."

I took his cup from him. He grabbed my hand. Pulled me to him. Our eyes met and our lips touched in a very gentle kiss.

"I like nosy neighbors." He said.

Still in shock I softly questioned, "You do?"

"I do." His smile was radiant.

I floated down the stairs.

The front door was open. I saw through the glass door... the day had turned sunny and a bit warmer. A walk was needed outside and around the house to see if there was any damage.

Stepping around the paraphernalia of the sleeping quarters from last night's storm... waited to be put away, I was determined not to let Mitch know how his remark hurt me, but it was true... I'd been nosy, but had my reasons. Funny, how the remark about Corbin and his different dates didn't seem to bother me as much... right now.

I walked outside and down the steps from the porch. Ethan, turned off the saw and removed his safety glasses.

With a grin he said, "Well... you have certainly had your share of surprises since last night. How's it going?"

Ethan was a handsome man and when he smiled it covered his entire face.

I grinned back. I was glad he was a friend, "I need to take a walk around and see if there's any damage."

"I checked it out for you. You're alright. This is a strong cottage, it's been here through many storms and I'm sure will remain for another hundred years."

"Thanks, Ethan. Mitch wants to know if you're interested in the downed trees on his property? He said he'd pay you."

"I'll take a look. He really took a shot— didn't he?"

"Yes and he's in pain. Through all of the commotion with Corbin, I discovered Mitch owns the company Corbin works for.

Not sure how that will float now. Corbin was a bit disrespectful to him." I ran my fingers through my hair. "I also learned, all the years he went to business functions, he took someone other than me. Nice guy... and he wanted to talk about the breakup. No way!"

By now Alex stood closer and said, "What a way to start a day. Ava told me about him. What's his name... Corbin? He's a real piece of work."

"Thanks, Alex. I know I'm not perfect... but he lacks so much and who knows... now his job may be in jeopardy. I'll probably get blamed for it too, like he always placed the guilt on me when it came to his clandestine activities."

Ethan and Alex worked most of the afternoon and cleared the huge tree from my lane. I kept a check on Mitch, he appeared to rest peacefully. A pot of red sauce was put on for dinner. I thought raviolis would be easy to chew. Maybe Mitch wouldn't be in quite as much pain.

I'd finally had the house straightened up and all of the storm gear put away. I occasionally stirred the sauce to make sure it thickened. Alex and Ethan left for the day. Ethan said he'd return tomorrow to check on me and see exactly what Mitch wanted to do about the fallen trees on his property.

I was busy with the sauce and tried to think what else might be good with dinner for Mitch to eat. I didn't want to cause him anymore discomfort. It was as if I felt his agony... with each thought of him.

There wasn't a sound, but a presence was felt behind me. I'd been deep in thought, when I felt arms wrap around my waist and a light kiss placed on my neck... I knew who it was. I was aware from his touch... it was Mitch. I turned slowly and was captivated by his eyes. If eyes could hypnotize, his had to be the ones.

"Kristen, I'm sorry about early today with Corbin. I shouldn't have told you about the other women... it wasn't my place. I couldn't allow him to change your mind. But, for all intents and purpose you did need to know. I realize now why he did what he did. You're owed an explanation."

"Mitch sit... I don't need you to pass out and hit the floor. Please sit."

He pulled out a chair for him and one for me, which he sat close to his. He was seated and pulled me to sit across from him. He held my hands in his. His eyes continued to hold me captive, yet made me feel tranquil.

"Kristen... to be fair to Corbin, I have to tell you why he never brought you to any of the company's activities. It was known you were taken with Windward Manor since you were a child... he knew how much research you'd done to find who owned it. I'd told him about the work I was prepared to do on the place once I took ownership. This had been about three years ago. He was aware I owned Windward Manor and if he'd brought you to New York and we were introduced... the name would ring a bell, questions would be asked and you'd have become involved to find answers ... he'd lose you. Furthermore I believe he knew once I saw you—I'd never stop with a pleasant acknowledgement."

"I... don't know what to say. Did you know who I was?"

"No... he's never mentioned you. I didn't realize until today Corbin knew you. He kept his relationship with you concealed.

Once you moved back here he had to know we'd meet and tried to move you back to San Francisco before it ever happened … before you knew who I was."

"He cheated on me more than once. I found out about it. It hurt me, it degraded me… why would he think I'd allow him to continue with this type of treatment?" I implored.

"Because now I've met you… I know why." He paused and squeezed my hands tightly. "He didn't want to lose you… especially not to me."

I asked innocently, "Why… and not to you?"

"Because, he's often said, what a lucky bastard I am to have it all. I don't have it all… I lost my father… my mother left us because my father worked many long hours, and left us alone. What I do have is my grandmother and the education I needed to expand the business—which was all I had, until I inherited the manor… and now I've met you." His expression was completely serious… he continued to hold my hands in his.

"I have to ask, Mitch, what does our encounter, have to do with any of this and Corbin?"

"One—I'm fascinated not only with your beauty, but with your kindness, compassion, and empathy. You didn't know me and I wasn't nice to you, but you took me in and have assisted me in more ways than one. Corbin recognized these qualities in you. He was aware of who you were… losing you forever, and possibly to me was too much for him. But he did cheat on you and I don't think he would have stopped, because it was in his nature. Kristen… I don't know where this may lead, or even if you sense the same things I do… but I can say I feel desire for you… much like our destiny. I can't lose you."

I was shocked by what Mitch said to me, I couldn't find the words to respond the way I wanted. He saw the confusion written on my face, but he needed to know I felt the same way.

I slid my hand from his and softly touched the side of his face. Ran my fingertips down its length—followed the line of his jaw, and his very sexy, much needed shave, "I'm sorry you're in pain— but I'm happy you're here with me."

He moved his face closer to mine, when our lips touched—I knew what he meant about destiny. All the years... curiosity about the manor, the people, and their lives—I truly knew I belonged somehow to him and Windward Manor, although we needed to discover the unknown...

Chapter 21

I felt better since Kristen knew my thoughts about her and almost sure she recognized we belonged together. I had a lot on my plate right now, needed to feel better, and return to New York. There was a problem which required my attention. Containers had disappeared from the ship when it left Port of Virginia the day of the storm.

I didn't want to leave her or the house. My biggest desire was to find answers to the mystery which surrounded the manor.

I've always been busy and never minded, but now I wanted to spend more time with Kristen... get to know her. Women come and go in my life, because I'd want them to move on. I never took an interest in anyone... not like I have... her.

Corbin was right not to bring her to New York to introduce us. I tried to ignore her and send her from me, but it didn't work. How to explain the effect she has on me, except to say, it's like learning to breathe again when you thought you'd taken your last breath, or to see something for the first time and know you purely had to have it. When her grey eyes would meet with mine, I couldn't wait to get close enough to touch her, and press my mouth to hers.

I made Mitch comfortable in the living room so he wouldn't have to climb the stairs again until after dinner. He asked if I could take him home. I didn't want him away from me. He needed to be watched.

"I must grab my razor to shave." He ran his hand along his jaw. "I'm not used to this unshaven look, plus — my laptop to check on business. I know... I should rest and promise to after you help me acquire a few items."

We'd talk after dinner. Mitch needed to explain exactly what it was he did. I had questions, but was aware it was related to container shipments, because of Corbin's job.

He was asleep. I sat down next to him on the couch with my hand lightly on his chest. "Mitch... dinner's ready. Are you hungry?" Just to feast on his relaxed, beautiful features stirred a hunger in me I'd never felt for Corbin.

His blue eyes opened. I felt, love, trust, and affection for him.

He pulled me closer and whispered, "I don't ever want to let you go."

The kiss which followed filled every corner of my heart.

"Mitch... I had to come back... to find you." I replied.

He began to sit up. I helped to pull him with my hand in his. We walked quietly to the kitchen. Before we sat down... he kissed me again.

"Something smells delicious," he said "You've been in this kitchen all day? After dinner you need to sit with me and relax."

Dinner was served and cleaned up. It was time for Mitch to take another pain and anti-biotic pill.

"Kristen, before you give me those pills, we need to go to

the house?" He gave me a big smile and added, "I also need to pack clean clothes."

It was dark by now and I needed to help Mitch with his request to gather a few items.

Was the light in the manor's upstairs window... lit? I wasn't about to look.

"If you feel up to going with me, Mitch... we can go now, or you can tell me where to find what you need and you can wait here?"

He stood and gathered me into his arms and said, "Until we find out what's going on in my house... I'll not permit you to go by yourself. I'm fine, we'll go together. It won't take long."

I put on my coat. Mitch said he'd be okay for the short ride without his. The inside and outside lights from my house were turned on to give us a glimmer of light through the trees, which were left rooted... and when we reached the manor we could hopefully see.

Ethan must have removed the large limb which had fallen on Mitch. He trimmed a few of the branches to better clear the way for a car to maneuver through. I pulled close to the house in the circular drive, parked the car, and we both climbed out.

Mitch wanted me to stay in the car, but he'd need my help. I wasn't fearful of the house. It was certainly questionable with its mysterious events... and of course when the key was placed in the lock... all of the lights came on.

With my hand in his and the astonished expression on his

face, I said, "Mitch, the house is welcoming me. I've waited almost twenty-one years to see if the house inside looks anything like the dreams I've had for years... maybe I belong here."

He questioned what I'd said.

"Okay we'll see. But why did I become injured?" He inquired.

"Would you have come to my house... stayed with me if the limb hadn't fallen on your head?" I asked.

He appeared surprised to hear me voice this opinion and grinned as he realized I could have been right.

"Well no... because I had so many other things on my mind." He replied honestly.

I laughed, "So—maybe the limb helped along the meeting?" I responded.

"Oh... like a wakeup call. Okay, let's see what happens?" He said with a smile.

The lights stayed on and we had the items he'd need for a few more days, along with his laptop. We left the house. It wasn't until we drove away, the lights went off.

"I don't know, Kristen... it's the weirdest thing I've ever encountered. My grandmother needs to be asked if she was conscious of any ghostly encounters when she lived here? I'm not sure what the connection is between you, me, and this house?"

Chapter 22

M itch was in the shower, he needed to keep his sutures dry. His medication was ready, his pillows fluffed against the headboard to sit and check his laptop until he became drowsy.

I needed to shower, but I wanted to make sure he was okay first. He came out of the bathroom appeared fresh and possibly felt a bit better.

He'd shaved and must have splashed on intoxicating cologne, it smelled divine. He was refreshed and appeared comfortable in his pajama bottoms and robe.

"Mitch, get yourself settled. It's my turn to shower and when I'm finished, you can fill me in on your business. Take your medicine, its right here… with a drink of water." I said.

"Sure, I want to tell you about the business. I'm going to contact my grandmother. You may want to hear what she has to say. I'll take the pills when you finish your shower… unless you want me to be asleep?" He inquired.

He gathered me to him, gave me a kiss and said, "Hurry back."

My hair could wait until morning to wash. The day had been too chaotic to shower this morning, because Mitch needed to be seen by a doctor, then Corbin, Ethan, Alex, also the time it took to make, and serve meals. I'd be quick and wondered what my life would be like with Mitch? I knew with the way I felt about him, it could only be *wonderful*. Was I making an assumption about him...us...too early? *I didn't think so.*

I was snuggled in my fluffy robe and started for his bedroom. When I reached the hall Mitch called to me from the window seat.

He eyed me with question and said, "Look... the light is on again in the upstairs room."

I stood behind him, my hand on his shoulder and took a peek. The room in the manor was lit by its usual soft glow.

"I'm calling my grandmother, there has to be more to this story," he said.

We went into the guest room. Mitch moved to the center of the bed with one pillow behind his back and gave me the other one. I hugged it to my chest while I sat to listen to the conversation he'd have with his grandmother. Mitch, seated in an upright position made the call... the phone was on speaker.

She answered.

"Gran, I have a few questions for you?" Mitch said.

"Hello, Mitch. How are you?" She sounded a bit miffed.

"Sorry, Gran. How are you?"

"I'm fine, what can I help you with?"

"First off..." He took a second. "You're on speaker so Kristen can hear. She may also have something to say."

"Who is Kristen... Mitch?" It was said with authority.

Mitch went into how we met and his grandmother was upset to think he'd been injured. We assured her he was well taken care of. After I was casually introduced over the phone and explained the events, and the lights, Mitch explained about the lights again.

She listened closely and then said with a preposterous tone, "I don't remember any incidents like these. I do remember your grandfather telling me about a secret room." She paused for a second. "I was all over the house when I first arrived as a domestic, and never found a secret anything. I thought it was all hogwash. This sounds like hogwash too. Are you sure there is no one living there you're not aware of? It is... a big house."

Mitch responded a bit aggravated, "No grandmother, there is no one else in the house."

"Well, Mitch... I can't help you. I have no idea what you and your friend are seeing."

"Thanks, Gran. We hoped you could shed a little light on the situation." He smiled at me, "No pun intended."

"How well do you know this... Kristine?" She asked.

Mitch's tone changed, "It's Kristen... and she's taking good care of me. Without her help... I don't know where I'd be. I'll see you next week. I have the container coming by boat this Friday with the rest of my furnishings. Thank you."

"Mitch... don't get uppity with me. I'm asking for your own good." She reacted.

"Grandmother, I'm old enough and wise enough at the age of thirty-two to know...

"To know what, Kent Mitchell Savage... you're not being taken advantage of? I certainly hope so! Because it sounds like someone is playing games with you... and that house! I told you I didn't like it there!" She sounded irate. "Now I know you'll never get me to go back!"

"Okay. Calm down. I'll see you next week." He said in a appeasing tone.

Mitch selected end on the phone.

I removed myself from the bed.

He grabbed my hand with a look of concern on his face.

"Where are you going?" He asked.

I turned slightly to view him, "To read a book," I answered pleasantly.

"Oh no you don't... not so fast, you're not going anywhere. You wanted to know about my company and I don't want you to leave." He pleaded.

Mitch took his medication and began to tell me about the company his father started and how he grew it into what it was today.

"It's a shipping company, it's a system known as intermodal freight transport—using cargo containers."

He said he shipped freight around the world and had offices in many ports in the U.S, abroad, and told me more about the origin of containerization. How it began in the coal mining regions of England in the late 18th century. In the 1830's railroads began the use of containers and now it was huge in the shipping industry.

I knew his heritage was English and his early relatives began the steamboats or ferry's from here to Virginia.

"So this is why you need to locate the containers you've lost in Virginia during the storm? Do you lose many containers?" I inquired.

"Only a few. Like when there are wicked storms, or if they're stacked too high, and not properly loaded. I have my own ships... we try not to overload. This is one reason I have someone in charge at each port and what Corbin's job was in San Francisco, Oakland, Long Beach, and Los Angeles. He checks the ports for arrivals and departures in California and makes sure it all runs smoothly. We are KSS Logistics, LLC International Shipping."

I needed to ask, "Is this why you had the bay dredged in front of your property?"

"Yes, I'd bought furniture and accessories in different areas of the country. This was the best means to transport them. It's only one container and will be placed on a small barge in the Port of Virginia, brought here to the new pier, and the container emptied."

I knew Mitch's medicine began to kick in because he began to yawn.

"Mitch, why don't you try and sleep, you need your rest." I said.

He smiled and said, "Will you sleep next to me... you did last night?"

I laughed and shrugged my shoulders. "I did, but we only had one bed to sleep on."

"We'll pretend we only have one bed tonight." He whispered sensually, "Lay with me, Kristen. I need to know you're here."

I laid our pillows flat and Mitch moved over. I climbed in next to him. We were tired and hadn't gotten much sleep last night with the storm, and waking him to make sure he'd be okay. I too thought I could sleep better next to him—than in my room. He turned to kiss me goodnight. Rolled on his side and drew me into the curve of his body. We fit nicely together.

I was relaxed, comfortable, and fell into a restful sleep.

Chapter 23

I woke and found myself alone. Where was Mitch and why didn't I hear him? I jumped out of bed to find him. The bag with his clothes we'd picked up last night was no longer in the bedroom.

I heard voices, they weren't loud, but distinctive. I put on my robe and headed towards the stairs. By the time I reached the third step, I saw Mitch fully dressed, coat, and all, in a discussion with Ethan. Down the stairs I went, opened the storm door, and out to stand on the porch.

"Good morning. Is this a conference I've been omitted from?" I questioned.

They both looked at me. Mitch pulled me next to him. It was cold, but my fluffy robe was pulled tightly around me and Mitch's arms kept me warm.

"Everything okay?" I asked.

Mitch answered, "Not necessarily. But before I leave I wanted to check with Ethan to see if he'd take care of the trees and a few other things for me. Thanks, Ethan. You have my number… if any problems arise call me." Mitch said.

Ethan saluted me and walked off with his chain saw in his hand. I was pushed gently back inside. There wasn't what I'd consider a smile on Mitch's face, but a distressed expression.

"What's going on, Mitch? Why are you leaving?" I asked.

"I didn't want to wake or disturb you. My phone vibrated early this morning and you were asleep... like Sleeping Beauty. I wasn't going to leave without a goodbye, but there are numerous freight problems which need my immediate attention in New York."

I stepped away from the warmth of his body. My arms folded in front of me I inquired, "Mitch... you're not driving... are you?" I was troubled.

He looked mysteriously at me, "I was. Why?" He asked.

He heard the worry in my voice when I said, "You can't, you were to rest, you have a concussion, and could pass out..."

"I'll be fine. I'd fly, but my plane is in use by one of my managers in Miami."

I became upset and disagreed adamantly, "No. No... I'll drive you to the airport. You'll take a commercial flight. Your grandmother doesn't like me now. If I let you drive she'd hate me— especially if something happened to you. I'll make us breakfast. You turn on your laptop and find a flight."

He smiled, "You're worried about me?"

"Well yes. I didn't stay up the night before last for naught."

He laughed and pulled me close, "Good morning Sleeping Beauty and you are beautiful even when you're asleep."

He kissed me a long and provocative kiss, not the gentle kisses like before. I could have melted like hot wax... right where I stood. We parted slightly... I asked what he'd like for breakfast. His baby blues lit up with his smile.

"It's a good thing I'm fully dressed and just about ready to leave." Were his words.

"Yeah. I think so too." Was my reply. "How about...coffee, eggs, toast and sausage?"

His face lit into a smile, "Sounds good, I'm not so sure I'll have another chance to eat for some time." He replied.

He looked wonderful dressed in his business suit. When I saw him at my door, he dripped wet with blood in a steady flow down his face, on his white shirt and tie. Big difference today... he looked better than... merely fine.

I served breakfast and ran upstairs to shower quickly. I had time to wash my hair. His flight wasn't for four hours, which gave me an hour to shower, dress and an hour to get him to BWI. He'd reach New York the same time as if he'd driven.

We traveled to the airport. I asked him what Ethan was to do for him besides take care of the trees.

He viewed me from the passenger's seat and answered, "Remember, I told you about the container to arrive on Friday with my possessions. I need him to oversee the removal of those items. Would you mind possibly, when the pieces come out of the container... to place them where I might like and where you think they should go?"

His judgment was the furniture bequeathed to and passed down were mostly antiques, but none of it was comfortable to sit or sleep on, only to be used as accents.

I took my eyes off the road for a second, "Mi... Mitch, how will I know where you want the furniture?"

He smiled, "I'm sure you'll know. "He said.

I thought I knew from my dreams. How ironic he also seemed to think I'd know.

He began to sound apologetic, "You have the shop to open on Saturday and Sunday. I hope to be back before then. Only do what you can, Kristen."

"I've only recently seen the two rooms off the hall from the door which led to the pool outside... and your bedroom."

"Be nosy and look at the rest of the house."

He reminded me which room was the master bedroom and if I wanted to search for the secret room, to give it a try.

We'd reached the airport. I drove to the passenger departure area.

"You can leave me off here." He looked long and hard at me. I had to ask, "Will you be okay?"

He leaned across the seat, touched the side of my cheek softly, pulled my face closer to his, and kissed me deeply.

His eyes searched mine. "I'll call you when I land." He handed me his house and car keys.

"Be careful, Mitch. Try to rest. Don't forget to at least take your antibiotic and don't worry about the container. Ethan, and I can handle it." I affirmed.

He kissed me a quick kiss, grabbed his bag off the back seat, and watched until I drove away. There were tears in my eyes.

In two days he'd reached every crack and crevice of my heart.

Upon return to my house Jeanette was there with Ethan. They'd had lunch on my front porch. I climbed out of the car and ran to where they were seated.

"Come inside. It's warmer." I said.

They followed me inside, "So how was your houseguest?" She asked.

"Jeanette… he was… is wonderful." I said, with a grin.

"Oh my… could this be love?"

I responded, "I know you'll say it's too soon, but man… it sure feels like it."

She and Ethan laughed and Jeanette said, "Never too soon. I knew when I met Ethan. It does happen."

I laughed, "I hope so… if it's not, life has passed me by."

Ethan spoke up, "There is always, Corbin."

"No! Thanks, but no thanks."

Ethan finished his lunch. Jeanette stayed to chat while he cut more of the fallen trees.

I was alone again and wanted to change the linens on the bed we'd slept in last night. Mitch's pillow was pulled to my face… his cologne inhaled. I hugged his pillow to me and my phone rang.

"My feet are on the ground and I miss you already."

"I miss you too. Was your flight delayed? It's night, Mitch."

"No, but once I landed all hell broke loose. Sorry this was the first chance I've had to call you, but you were on my mind. Did you go to the house and look for the hidden room."

"I wanted to, but Jeanette was here when I returned from the airport. She'd brought lunch for Ethan and when he went back to work we sat and talked. By the time she left it was almost dusk and the sun was low on the water. I know all the lights would have been on… but I'll wait until tomorrow."

"Please be careful. I'm still not convinced the spirit is friendly." He added.

"I'll be fine, how are you?" I asked.

"I'm tired. Thoughts are I should stay at my grandmother's at least tonight. She's concerned about my injury, but I don't agree with her assumption of you. You do know I kind of like you… more than a little."

I laughed, "Yeah…I got it. Do you know I feel the same way."

"I hoped you did. Call me anytime tomorrow. I'll take your calls… to hear your voice as often as I can… while I'm away."

"You can call me too. My thoughts are with you, Mitch." I reminded him.

"I'll be dreaming about you, baby. Bye." He said.

I didn't want to put the phone down. How many days did I have to wait for him to return? If he returned on Friday I'd only have Wednesday and Thursday.

God… please make the days go by fast.

Chapter 24

I pulled into the circular drive of Windward Manor. Ethan was hard at work on the fallen trees. He saw me when I climbed out of my car.

"Hey... what's up?" He inquired.

"I'm in search of a secret room. Want to come along and hunt with me? I've been dying to see the inside of this house since we were kids." I said enthusiastically.

"I know you have, but it may be ghostly inhabited from what I hear. Are you sure you want to do this?" He probed.

"Well, Ethan, we have to be in here on Friday anyway until Mitch gets back. Come on, we'll stick close together."

He shrugged his shoulders and sat down his saw, "Okay. Why not?"

We both laughed and mounted the stairs in front of the stone mansion. They were wide and low, we approached the double wide, carved, wooden front door. I placed the key in the lock and the door swung open.

Ethan drew back, "Whoa... wasn't the door locked?"

"Yes. It was, but this house seems to greet me. It's as if I belong here." I said.

His expression was one of a pessimist, "You really believe this, Kristen?" He pondered.

"I do. I've watched and admired this house since I was

five. Maybe before then, but I don't really remember. Twenty-one years... well no... I was gone for eight of those years, but it knows how much I love it. Come on, stay with me you'll be okay." I responded.

He raised his brow and smiled, "Years ago... I used to say the same to you when we'd play and you'd be afraid to go where we weren't allowed. I guess you trusted me. I'll have to trust you."

We began in the main hallway. The rooms were huge. The moldings were beautiful and the floors had been refinished. The twelve foot ceilings made the rooms appear the size of a ballroom, which I was sure at least one was— in the day. There was a smaller room or parlor freshly painted with refinished floors.

Through an enormous room was another hallway and led into the downstairs wing with a huge parlor and stairway which lead to a group of rooms, one of them was where I'd see the soft glow of light when it became dark.

I wasn't ready to go up there until I finished downstairs.

Behind the massive downstairs room was a portion of the kitchen, which ran the length of the back of the house, it looked to have been renovated from its pantry, prep, cook, and eat in area. It was mammoth. All stainless steel appliances, an eight burner stove and several ovens.

We walked the length of the kitchen which came back into the main hallway to the double French doors which led to the outside pool area. To the right of the hallway was what appeared to be the library—study combination with its mahogany panels along three sections of the walls and its wide entryway to divide the room.

Through the far doorway was the entrance to the right wing

of the house with steps which led upstairs. I wasn't sure what this room would be used for, but the view of the bay from the flow of windows on the adjacent walls—was magnificent. I thought the panels in the library-study may have concealed the secret room along with all of the mahogany bookshelves.

Ethan and I walked back to the main foyer and began to climb the wide, spiral, cherry staircase to the upstairs.

"I cannot imagine what in the world Mitch will do with all of this space. I think the one enormous room has to be the dining room since it's connected to the kitchen. What do you think?" He asked me.

"I think you're right, Ethan. Before his furniture arrives, I better know which rooms are for what, so we know where to place the furniture. It seems each one has a huge chandelier… it makes it hard to decipher."

We reached the top of the stairs and Ethan said, "Each of the men in the portraits… their appearances are impressive."

"You could say that, they all resemble one another except for their attire."

The upstairs hallway did not go into the other two sections of the house. I guess those rooms could only be reached by the other two stairways from the downstairs.

There were four enormous bedrooms upstairs, each with its own bathroom, but I already knew which one was the master suite. Not only because it held some of Mitch's personal possessions, but the scent and aroma of his delicious cologne lingered in the air and I'd been here when we came to gather his clothes.

There was a four poster king size bed. My thoughts drifted to a night in this bed… next to him. The image alone sent chills up my spine and my heart seemed to beat to its own rhythm.

The large armoire and a high chest were made of mahogany. They looked lost in the vastness of the room.

I knew each of the upstairs rooms had been complemented with bathrooms, when the renovation was completed.

Once Ethan and I came down the stairs, with an awareness to see what the upstairs in the two other wings looked like, was intense. I went to the far right wing first, took the stairs to the room above. It was one large room, with a long bar, already fully stocked. This would be for enjoyment and the view of the bay was incredible. There was a small kitchen behind the bar area and an elevator which took us downstairs, its door opened behind the staircase.

Now it was time to view the upstairs room which observed my home. I didn't think I ever mentioned this to Ethan. If I had... I'd forgotten. I'll see what he has to say once we see the room.

Now the jitters became apparent to me while we climbed the stairs slowly... using the excuse I was worn-out. This section of the house was being refurbished. Faded and worn wallpaper remained on most of the walls. There was one large bathroom and three bedrooms, and only one room... which contained a sitting area... and overlooked... my domain.

I didn't sense any ethereal presence. The room was empty as were all the rooms in this wing. There were no ceiling lights or candles, but the lone window looked into the center hall of my home. The only other window in the room... looked out towards the bay.

We started downstairs when Ethan said, "I never noticed the side window before. The abundance of previous trees must have hidden it."

I told him they must have... because I could see it now.

"Ethan... I've been curious and I haven't been honest with you. I always see a light in this room."

"Kristen, I can't believe you came up those steps, into the room, and didn't say a word to me about a light. But there wasn't a thing in there."

"I know... it's too weird. Mitch saw it too, not just me. Well no one got us." I giggled, "I guess we're safe. Did you feel anything ghostly in any of the rooms?"

"Well there were cold spots." He laughed. "But this house is so damn big and it's cold out—so no—nothing cataclysmic."

"Ethan, after what we've viewed on each floor, where would you think the hidden room would be." I quizzed.

He shook his head, "Got me, Kristen... maybe in one of the closets. We didn't really check them."

We were on our way to the front door. "You know... I think I'll wait for Mitch." I said. "He and I can go over this house, one room at a time."

"So, Kris... you've really fallen for him. Do you think you could live here?"

I was serious when I turned to him and said, "I could, Ethan... I really could."

Chapter 25

E than went back to cutting the fallen trees and I went home.
There was quite a bit of daylight left before it grew dark.
Today was Wednesday and I'd placed a call earlier to Mitch, but
was told he was in a conference and my call would be returned
later.

It was later. I'd have to be patient. He was busy and probably
wasn't feeling normal. I prayed he didn't work too hard.

Ethan stacked piles of wood, and had been told to sell what
he could and keep the money. Mitch only wanted two cords to
season for next year. He'd already bought a supply of firewood.

I debated about the wood not sure where I'd spend most
of my time, but began to reconsider in case the electric went
off—the fireplace would help to keep the pipes from freezing,
since I'd spent a lot of money renovating.

Friday the container would arrive. Ethan needed assistance.
He'd asked a few of his friends who'd helped him expand the
outside deck on the Crab Shanty. It seemed once summer was

over and we were into the beginning of November, odd jobs
were needed to supplement the winter incomes.

Jeanette found a job at the Urgent Care Facility where Mitch
had been taken. She started her job today. Cory was in school
and Ethan liked to stay busy. To cut wood, oversee, and empty
the container would help. Plus Mitch paid well.

I busied myself on the computer and placed an inventory
order for the shop. Halloween had passed and Thanksgiving
and Christmas were just around the corner. Displays for each
holiday were important for sales. While on the computer I
looked at items for both holidays and couldn't wait to decorate
the store with my exclusive inventory.

Mitch would drift into my thoughts.

I hadn't spoken to him since last night when he arrived in
New York and by now it was almost dinner time. He said call
anytime, but I wasn't going to become a pain in his tail.

After I saw the interior of his house—I began to think
where someone would hide a secret room. It had to be in the
main house and not in the wings. They were built years later.

My phone finally rang, it had to be Mitch.

"Hello, I've been worried about you." I said.

"I've thought about you too." He responded, "But I have
bad news."

I'd already begun to panic and was concerned, "Mitch,
what's happened? Are you okay... please... tell me you're all
right?" I implored.

"I'm okay... still have headaches, but I'm sure they will

eventually go away, and when these sutures are removed I'll have to feel better. How are you?" He asked.

"Fine... I miss you and can't wait until Friday." Was my response. Then I asked kiddingly, "Is there a cook who comes with the big kitchen?" I laughed slightly. "Ethan and I went through the house, it's beautiful. It's every bit as exclusive as I thought it would be."

"Kristen... the bad news is... I won't be home Friday. There are many lost containers. We're trying to locate and place them where they belong. Someone tried to sabotage my operation."

He sounded browbeaten. I wish I was closer to at least give him a hug.

"This has never happened before, we've had one conference after another to sort this out, and figure what could have gone wrong. The containers in Virginia from the storm have been located, but there's no reason for the other containers to be misplaced. We're not sure if they are lost at sea or not shipped. It's a big mess. I'm sorry, but until we get this confusion straightened out, I don't know when I'll be back. If you don't know where to put the items from the container on Friday, just set them anywhere for now. When I return I'll figure it out. Got to go— I'll try to call later."

Besides the problems Mitch faced, he sounded different. He didn't say we'd figure it out, but he'll figure out where to put the furniture.

Maybe he thought we were too hasty and rushed the situation between us, or perhaps... I've read too much into his hurried phone call.

I needed to give him a break. I'm sure owning a huge corporation when strange circumstances happen... he'd undoubtedly be preoccupied. I'll sit tight until I'd hear from him again.

This would be a long night for me. I wouldn't be able to think of anything but him and wasn't as excited about my order of holiday inspired items... now the thrill was gone.

It was dark outside and dinner became obsolescent. I went upstairs to the room where we'd slept... now sorry I'd changed the sheets. There wasn't a trace or a slight suggestion of his cologne. He was gone—and I was miserable.

To sit in the hallway and gaze upon the soft glow of light from the manor gave me comfort... it appeared to beckon to me. There had to be a connection somewhere with the light, house, and me.

Chapter 26

The days went by slowly. No word from Mitch since Wednesday. There wouldn't be time for me to call him this morning. I was up early to keep watch for the arrival of the container.

I sat alone in the cold on the stone wall of the manor and observed the horizon for the powered barge. Finally... it was within my sights and made its slow approach. Ethan was contacted and on his way.

The container holding Mitch's possessions was attached to the barge, and tied tightly to the dock's massive pilings with the captain's help. Now I knew why he'd had the new dock constructed.

Ethan had Simon and Will to help him. I was to remain inside the house and direct them as each piece of furniture was carried in. My wish was to have most of the furniture arranged for Mitch. It would be a surprise for him.

I hadn't attempted to enter the house until Ethan arrived. Even though I said, the house seemed to welcome me... I was a bit wary of going inside alone.

Ethan and I walked across the stone patio to the wide

double French doors. The key placed in the lock, and the doors opened—of their own accord.

We'd seen this before, but I don't think we'd ever be comfortable with it. There were latches to hold the doors in the opened position, but were not used. With the swift breeze off the bay, I thought the doors would waver... but they seemed fixed in place.

A smile and a glance of disbelief passed between Ethan and me.

Simon and Will arrived and the container had been opened. It was filled with furnishings. The quilts were taken from a few pieces of furniture... they'd be the first to be removed.

The first piece was a beautiful light pine, harvest table. My thoughts were the kitchen. It took all three of the men to carry it from the pier. It went perfect in the kitchen, a long bench, which matched was next.

It was easy to identify the chairs to match the table when they were unloaded. The set made the space homey and not seem big and cold.

Next to be unloaded had to be the dining room table. Once placed in the large room, it was opened and the four leaves were inserted. It was an excellent choice of mahogany for this location. Chairs were next, the sideboard, and finally a server.

It seemed Mitch or someone had packed and grouped the furniture together on a per room basis. Each piece designated its own position in the house.

The furnishings had been chosen specifically for each space. The rooms came together... even down to the jukebox in the bar, the bistro tables, and chairs. The pool table enhanced the area and established an announcement … it was a tavern. Possibly an English Pub. I'd never seen one, but once the red antique phone booth was in place, I'd say it was meant to be a pub.

There were boxes with dishes for the dining room and kitchen, pots, pans, other small, and useful appliances. The living room or ball room was enormous, and had not yet been unloaded, neither had the library combination study.

There were two such lovely benches of wrought-iron filigree for the front porch on either side of the wide door. The porch did not require a roof, but was long like the main house, made of stone, with the wide low steps, which made the approach to the front door effortless, yet gracious.

Large urns were placed by the front steps. After going onto the porch the front door was left unlocked, in case there were more entry accessories.

Three pizzas had been ordered and everyone stopped for lunch. I looked around at how beautifully the house came together. There were pictures, which needed to be hung, but would be Mitch's choice as to where. I'd hoped he'd be able to leave New York and join me. I didn't think I'd see him anytime soon and hadn't heard from him. It was sad he couldn't be here to see his home come together.

Once everyone had eaten, the guys uncovered and carried in more of the furniture for the upstairs bedrooms. This was harder for me to decipher, because the furniture could go in any one of the rooms. I'd make the decision and hope Mitch approved.

We were busy and moved about the house. I fussed over where I thought the hall table should be centered… out of nowhere the wind began to blow inside the house. The doors would open and slam shut. The house became a turmoil. An uncontrolled environment. I saw Ethan run. He shouted for me to go outside.

"Kristen, something has upset the house! Get out...get out of here!" He screamed.

The house had become unrestrained and cryptic. Chandeliers swayed and the lights flickered. I couldn't believe what was taking place. I turned to see which way to run.

When I turned, there stood Corbin in the foyer. *What... what was he doing here?* The house was not content upon his arrival. I heard him yell, "What the hell is going on here... Kristen? Get out of here."

I knew I was safe. It was him. He wasn't supposed to be here. I heard Ethan continue to holler for me. Corbin stood in one spot his hand extended to me.

I spun around again trying to figure out the best way to move beyond Corbin's reach. I... I saw Mitch. He stood at the front door, his stance out of character for him.

The house became quiet.

I watched in shock as Mitch walked up to Corbin and grabbed him by his collar.

"I knew it had to be you. You purposely messed with the shipments. You shipped containers where they weren't supposed to go and didn't ship those that needed to go. You did all of this to keep me away from, Kristen."

I'd never seen Mitch so infuriated. "You thought if you came here—with me in New York —you could get her to go back to San Francisco with you. You're fired Corbin and if Kristen wants to go with you..." I saw the fear in Mitch's eyes when he finished what he began to say, "You ask her now... in front of me... and see what answer she gives you. We both know you're a coward... a liar... and a cheat."

I was stunned to see Mitch, but more than shocked to know what Corbin had done to keep us separated. I walked to Mitch. He grabbed me around the waist and pulled me close.

Ethan now stood close enough to Corbin so if he had to seize him, I knew he would. "Go ahead, Corbin, ask Kristen again want she wants in front of me, she is free to choose."

The lights flickered. This is where I belonged not only in this house, but with Mitch. I'd never love Corbin the way I loved him... ever... and not in this short span of time.

"Corbin, I'm sorry you deceived Mitch to get to me, but I told you before... we are through. I'd never be able to love you again after all of your deceptions... or forgive you enough to marry you. I came back to Claiborne for a reason and the reason was to be with, Mitch. I'm in love with him."

Corbin finally spoke in a foul manner, "You didn't even know him when you came back, how can you say... you came back for him."

I defended myself as I screamed back at him, "This house... this house had a hold on me since I was a young girl. It's why I came back after you cheated on me. It drew me here to meet, Mitch. You saw how upset the house became when you entered and thought you'd harm me. It knew what you'd done to Mitch's business. This house has a spirit which has lived all of these years and waited for us. Leave and don't come back. I told you before you're not welcome."

"I can't believe... you have faith in what you've said to me. Do you really think this house knows if I wanted to harm either one of you? You're a fool, Kristen!"

Corbin turned to leave. When he neared the open front door it slammed so hard... it pushed him out of the house... he landed face down on the front porch. Ethan opened the door to watch him pick himself up and hobble off.

Mitch embraced me in a welcoming kiss.

"You know the last words Corbin said are true, I am a fool, Mitch... over you."

He held me tightly and said, "I'm glad you are, because I got here as fast as I could. I was afraid he'd hurt you. I'm a fool over you too. I love you, Kristen, if not more than this house does."

I hadn't left the safety of his arms and his kiss told me he loved me and we'd be happy here.

Will and Simon had moved a desk into the library. Mitch and I walked in together to see where it would be the most functional.

After they went to retrieve more furnishings... Mitch and I were alone.

I saw something.

"Mitch, the panel, the one panel on the wall between the ball room and here, look at it."

He walked slowly over to the section which was slightly ajar. He pulled on one corner and pushed on another. The panel, without hinges began to open wider. The look of surprise was on both of our faces. Stone steps about three foot high led into the secret room.

It wasn't immense but large enough to hold what appeared to be volumes of books and a few other items.

"Mitch, this would have been a safe place from water if the bay surged during a nor'easter or a hurricane to keep records safe and dry."

Mitch went after a flashlight and we stepped up into the room. There were what appeared to be wooden beds fastened to the walls. Something which resembled a wood burning stove, a way to heat water, was in one corner. There was a washstand consisting of a bowl and pitcher. There were chamber pots.

"Mitch… I read slaves were not used to farm this land, but do you think this house was part of the Underground Railroad? Harriet Tubman lived not far from here."

"Kristen, you could be right, but now, this minute, we don't have time to actually check out the books." Mitch held one of the books and flipped through it. "It's a ledger for the cost of supplies and profit from the crops." He picked up a second book and it revealed the same information. "We need to investigate what's here, but for now, let's close up this room. I want to get the container unloaded. I have to return to New York. I know you have to open your shop this weekend… but I'd like for you to come with me, meet my grandmother."

"Mitch, I'd like nothing better, but I don't know if I can… but I could leave Sunday after I close the shop and remain with you through the week?"

He reached for me and held me close, kissed me tenderly and said, "This will work. I'll go on ahead, take care of business, and be able to spend time with you."

We walked outside. He called to Ethan, "Ethan, can you keep, Kristen safe until Sunday evening?"

"I'm sure, Mitch…" He laughed and said, "If she stays here she'll be safe. I've never seen anything like I experienced today. No one will bother her in this house. But I'll make arrangements to keep her, with Jeanette and me."

I reminded Ethan I had to work and I hadn't used Brittany or Katie since business had been slow.

"Jeanette works on Saturday during the day and I'll have Cory. I'll get mom to work with you and then you're welcome to stay with us. Jeanette can help you in the shop on Sunday and we'll take you to the airport when the shop closes." He said.

I looked at Mitch he waited for my answer. "I'll need to pack sometime before Sunday evening."

Mitch spoke up, "Ethan, unload the rest of the furnishings and set them anywhere for now. I'll take Kristen home to pack and she can stay with you, go to work, and you can deliver her to the airport Sunday night. I think it will work." He looked at me again and I detected he was optimistic I'd agree… and I did.

Chapter 27

T he ledgers had been placed back into the secret room the panel pushed tightly shut before anyone was aware of what we'd found.

I was sure of why the secret room was exposed to us, "Mitch, the panel was opened to us on purpose. And the reason may be in one of those books. We need to investigate." I pleaded.

His look was thoughtful and after I'm sure he had a moment to consider he said, "I know you're right, sweetheart, but right now I have to go back to New York. I want you with me. I promise the following with Corbin out of the way, will enable me to get my business straightened out. We'll get to the bottom of this mystery related to the house, and the light when we return."

Mitch walked outside again and told Ethan we'd be back to lock up, but if we weren't... by the time he finished unloading the container to call. Mitch took my hand and we left by the front door. He drove me home in the rental car.

I focused on his profile and saw he had a lot on his mind. I didn't think he felt well. "Mitch..." I reached for his hand, held it tightly. "You need to rest. While I pack will you try to sleep? You didn't look around the house to see how nice it came together."

"I could use a nap… I was so worried and intent on reaching you before Corbin could harm you or steal you away. I didn't think of much else. He made such a mess out of the shipping schedule. When I realized it was to keep me in New York, and preoccupied with business… he hoped I wouldn't think about you. God… I was glad you were at Windward Manor when he arrived. I don't know what I'd have done if he'd injured you in some way, or forced you into leaving with him."

I squeezed his hand and he peered at me with his blue eyes which showed honesty and much stress.

I wanted to cry.

The car was parked on the side of my house in the designated area, and before we got out, he leaned in for a kiss. It was a sweet kiss, one which showed he'd been worried and was now somewhat relieved since Corbin was gone and hopefully out of our lives.

He was out of the car and came to open my door. I climbed out and began to plead with him, "Do you have to leave tonight. Can't you take an early flight tomorrow. You look like you need a good night's sleep." I expressed.

He pressed his body against mine in a way he hadn't done except when we were sleeping, "If I stayed tonight we wouldn't sleep… it's my jet, but scheduled to fly the new manager to San Francisco early tomorrow, so I need to be in New York tonight. The nap will have to do. I'll wait until Sunday night to be with you."

I knew from the look he gave me, we shared a moment to last forever. His lips met mine in passion this time. His tongue invaded my mouth and I felt my response to him. I wanted this sensation to go on endlessly... but knew he was rushed for time and we'd have to wait until Sunday.

I needed to pack for the week ahead.

We walked onto the porch hand in hand. He unlocked the door... turned the knob and we entered my home.

It made me think of the night not long ago when the wind, rain, and lightning were so horrendous I spent the night in the hallway when he pounded on my door. His hair soaked with rain and blood... both rolled down his exceptionally handsome face. When he came into the house, even though his disheveled appearance should have baffled me, one look into his blue eyes gave me pause. It took me a few seconds to realize he needed help... only I could give.

I pushed thoughts of how he treated me aside and could do nothing less than ask him in. My heart beat erratically at the sight of him... then... and now. He was taller than me by at least six inches, his hair dark, with it's tantalizing appearance. It was not short, but longer than what was considered moderately— well groomed. When uncombed it gave the appearance of windblown and sexy as hell. Those eyes were bluer than I've ever seen and not a dark blue, but an aquamarine blue. His wet shirt adhered to his perfect body, one that's seen mornings or evenings at the gym. Here he was again... he was tired and drained from his business, and thoughts for my safety.

I led him upstairs to the room we'd shared a few nights ago, removed the comforter and accent pillows, told him to rest, and I'd wake him soon, when I finished gathering my clothes for not only the weekend, but the week.

I wouldn't try to pack perfectly. When I reached Ethan's and Jeanette's, I'd straighten out my luggage. Mitch needed to be at the airport by six, his jet was scheduled to leave by seven. It was now almost three.

I'd no idea what to take. There were outfits I hadn't worn since I'd been home form San Francisco. They were clean and most would be perfect for casual or proper dinners and evenings in New York.

My style of dress had changed from a more formal style to beach casual... jeans and sweaters when it became colder in Claiborne.

For now I'd take the entire collection from San Francisco to Jeanette's and Ethan's, all I'd need to do was slide them into a garment bag, which folded in half for the flight to New York.

A gym bag was packed for what I'd need for work this weekend. My suitcase for New York would hold more casual items to wear, shoes and intimate apparel. The carry on would be for jewelry to be worn with outfits and other necessities.

I was ready and what may have been forgotten, I'd buy in New York. It was 4:30 p.m. Time to go. I hated to wake Mitch he looked so peaceful. Even with the section of his head shaved he was exceptionally handsome. His hair being a little longer covered most of the wound.

I walked lightly into the bedroom. Leaned across him to gently kiss his very sensual lips. He sensed me and grasped me to him.

"Kristen, I'm anticipating next week and our time together. There's so much I want to show you, but most importantly, is time spent together to learn more about this sensation of love I feel for you."

"I look forward to the same things. These last few days with you gone made me realize how much you mean to me in such a short period of time."

"I'm glad you feel it too. By the way... have you ever been to New York?" He asked with a beautiful smile.

"No, never, but look forward to it with you." I replied.

"Good... because I want you to see it all and enjoy every bit of it alongside of me. We'll stay at my place, but visit my grandmother's one evening. She's not happy about my need to live in Windward Manor, but I want to share my life with you there."

He saw the surprised expression on my face, but I was aware... what he said... he meant. I read it in his eyes.

He pulled me tightly to his chest, "You look surprised... is the realization I want you shocking to you? I don't want you for just an hour, a day, a week or a year, but a lifetime." His voice became softer, "Is it too much to ask?"

His sensual lips and he called for a response from me, "No, Mitch, it's what I want too."

My mouth found his this time.

Chapter 28

My luggage and gym bag were in Mitch's car and we were on our way to the manor. I hated the thought of his leaving, but I'd have Cory to brighten my weekend.

She was such a delight with her green eyes, like her mom's, and her wonderfully cute sense of self. Her strawberry blonde curls made her appear as though she should play the part of *Annie*.

I tried to avert my thoughts from Mitch and the strong feelings of love I had for him to what my weekend would be like with Ethan, Jeanette, and Cory. There was one thing to be thankful for... the items I'd ordered for inventory would not arrive until my return from New York.

We were in sight of the manor when Mitch ultimately noticed the wrought iron benches, and the huge urns on the porch.

"They look great, don't you think?" He said.

"Yes, I think once we plant a small ornamental tree or flowered plant in each one... it will be perfect."

He helped me from the car, stole another kiss, led me up the stone walkway, and steps. The front door was unlocked.

We entered.

In the last few hours the house began to look like a home.

The ball room or living room's furniture was in place, the table in the wide foyer, was not only in place, but had a vase filled with fall flowers. From the foyer I could see to the furnished parlor and dining room.

We looked at one another and couldn't comprehend how the entire ball of wax fell into place with the finishing touches… which had been added.

Ava appeared and walked into the foyer. Her smile was welcoming.

"Hello. We've been waiting for your return. Ethan informed Alex he was here to unload a container, and how you and Mitch left to pack for your weeks stay in New York. Jeanette was off from work and school was out for me… so we thought we'd come help. Hope you don't mind?"

"Mind… it looks wonderful."

I needed to make an introduction, "Mitch, this is Alex's wife, Ava, and Jeanette, must be close by."

Jeanette came into view arms extended, "I'm right here…" I gave her a hug and presented her to Mitch.

Together we walked through the hallway, to the back of the house. The boxes with kitchen supplies, small appliances had been opened, and waited to be put away.

Mitch said he was pleased to meet everyone and thanked them for being so helpful. I stayed inside with Ava and Jeanette, while he strode outside to see how much more remained in the container.

"Mitch, we're just about finished here, only a few more boxes and a few pictures. Then I think we're done. If you'd like… when you return from New York… I'm available if you need help to hang pictures."

"Thanks, Ethan, and thank you for your safe keep of my lady until Sunday. I look forward to the time I share this house and my life with her."

"Wow, you move fast, Mitch. I guess Kristen is aware of how you feel… because it's always been her dream, or should I say she was sure she would end up living in Windward Manor."

"She knows, and I knew the minute I laid eyes on her."

I watched Mitch intently as he spoke to Ethan when suddenly I heard, "Kristen, has he asked you to live here with him?"

I turned to look at Jeanette, "Yes, in so many ways and words. He's my destiny and so is this house."

She and Ava hugged me and said, "He seems perfect for you, Kris, plus he's so handsome you couldn't possibly have said no… without someone thinking you were crazy,"

The three of us had a hearty laugh.

Mitch entered the house. "Whose car should we unload your things into?" He looked at his watch and said, "Unfortunately I have to leave."

Jeanette had driven her vehicle, we went to move the items into her SUV. Once the transfer was completed, I stood with Mitch at the driver's side of his rental car.

We were wrapped in each other's arms… he kissed the side of my head and whispered, "Stay safe for me, I'll be in baggage claim waiting for you Sunday at 8:00 p.m. I'll take you to eat before we go home. I'm sure you'll be hungry."

I smiled up at him, "I'm hungry now, but it will have to wait."

"I know exactly what you mean." He beamed.

The kiss which followed said goodbye for now, but the promise it held... would be worth the wait.

"Kristen, I promise to call you when I land. I'd said the same words the last time, but because of certain circumstances I found it impossible... not this time. Missing you is like missing the air I breathe."

One last kiss and he slid behind the driver's seat, "By the way you have the keys to my car. Let Ethan use it to take you to the airport and maybe he'll pick us up when we return. If he can't and you want to drive yourself... and it's safe... which means you haven't heard from Corbin, then I can drive us home when we return."

"Okay. Have a safe trip. I'll see you Sunday, Mitch. I can't wait and don't forget to call."

I leaned into the car and captured his face in my hands and kissed him again. I stood and watched... he closed the window and waved as he drove off. A tear slid onto my check.

The iPhone was checked... on and charged. I slipped it back into my pocket wiped at my eyes... and entered the house.

The front door was locked this time. I didn't want any more surprises today. One scare was enough. My friends waited for me. They both placed an arm across my shoulders and led me to the kitchen. We sat at the harvest table, which now held a large bowl in its center, and one day... not next week, but the one after... would be filled with fresh fruit.

Ethan entered and said, "That's it, everything's unloaded

and hopefully in its precise place. My question is, who will cook in this kitchen? It's larger than mine at the Crab Shanty."

"You know I asked the same question, but never received an answer. Maybe it will be me? Great place to prepare for a large crowd." I laughed.

Ethan gave a chuckle along with, Ava and Jeanette.

The thought came to me, this was to be my home, "I want to walk through one last time, and then I'll be ready to leave. Oh! I just thought of something, we loaded my luggage into your SUV Jeanette, and I have Mitch's keys to his car and my car's here too."

"It's okay, why don't you let Ava drive your car home Kristen, you follow her in Mitch's car, park yours and then you both come back to our house in his. Ethan received a shipment of crabs today and there aren't any customers, so we'll have steamed crabs for dinner, and Alex will join us." Jeanette said.

"Okay… sounds great. I have containers of homemade crab soup in the freezer I'll bring them. I also have ice cream and garnishes for sundaes I'll donate. Crabs, soup, and dessert… we're all set." I announced happily.

Chapter 29

Jeanette was almost ready to serve dessert when my phone rang. It was Mitch.

"My jet isn't ready, some minor problem and I'm here alone with visions of you."

"I hope they were good ones." I laughed." I'm glad you had the chance to take a nap, did you eat?"

"I did and those images of you couldn't have been more perfect. I needed to hear your voice. It might be late when we land, would you still want me to call?"

"Yes, I'll be awake. I'm settled at Ethan's and Jeanette's, we're ready to prepare sundaes, we had crab soup, and steamed crabs for dinner... but they didn't compare to my thoughts of you."

"I can say the same, but I think your dinner may have been better. I need to try steamed crabs when I get back to town. I've heard so much about them, but haven't had the opportunity to indulge. Hold on a sec." I heard him talking to someone, he came back on the phone. "Okay flight check has passed, we're on our way. Love you, babe. I'll call you later."

"Ditto. Have a safe flight." There was that damn tear again. Come on Sunday.

Jeanette asked if I was okay. I told her I was. Mitch called. She looked at her watch, "He's there already?"

"No, his flight was delayed seems there was a minor problem, he's taking off now." I replied.

Everyone became quiet. I'm sure they were waiting to hear more, but at this time there was no more to say.

The ice cream had been dipped and everyone topped the ice cream with their choice of trimmings. Cory was excited since she was allowed to put chocolate and whipped cream on her sundae.

Dinner and dessert were over. The day had been long and I wanted to be in bed and wait for Mitch's call. Jeanette and Ethan's new house was quite a change from my older home. Everything smelled new. I hung my garment bag in the closet and was thankful not only to have my longtime friend back, but also have his wife as my comrade.

Cory was headed to bed and asked if I'd tuck her in and tell her a story. I made it a short story, but it was the story of a young girl who wanted to live in the manor house on the bay. And now I could say my story has come true... not dreams anymore. But the mystery surrounding the home needed to be solved. I left this part out. She fell asleep before I finished. She was either tired or my story bored her.

Jeanette asked if Cory realized the girl in the story was me. "No, and I didn't tell her which house. I made it sound like a fairytale... and to me it is."

"Go to bed and relax. I think we're ready to turn in for the night too." She said.

"Thanks, Jeanette. I appreciate your hospitality. Your house is beautiful."

"Thank you for the help to choose all the great finds and

make it our home. It was fun. You earned your stay." We both laughed and said goodnight.

I looked at the time and knew Mitch would soon call. I washed my face, brushed my teeth, and changed for bed. I climbed between the fresh sheets and waited for my phone to ring.

It wasn't long after I was snuggled in bed, Mitch called. It was wonderful to hear his voice. He was on the tarmac with his feet safely on the ground… and was tired. This had been a long day for him. A limo waited… he didn't have to drive.

We talked on his ride home about the house and he finally answered my much earlier question about the kitchen and a cook.

"It does come with a cook. I expect you to spend more time with me since we'll have our very own chef." He added.

"That won't be a problem for me, but I'd like to prepare you a meal or two."

"I also like to cook. The kitchen is big enough for three… four… or more," he responded.

We laughed and spoke of how we felt about each other and how he couldn't wait until Sunday night. Of course I couldn't wait either. I yawned and so did he, it was time to say goodnight, tomorrow would be a busy day for both of us.

"Kristen, if there are any problems with Corbin, please call me and the police. He will be held on charges of harassment and sabotage."

"Please try to get some sleep, Mitch. Call me tomorrow… when you have time." I asked.

"I promise… I'll make time. I need to hear your voice to

keep me going. Oh and by the way… stay away from Windward Manor until I'm with you. We'll research the books and ledgers together. Love you… bye."

We hung up. I knew I'd fall asleep in no time—I was exhausted.

Chapter 30

J eanette and I were up early. She had to work today. Cory was asleep and Ethan was at the Crab Shanty. He waited on a seafood delivery. Simon and Will were needed to work until Ethan could return home for Cory.

"Jeanette, call Ethan and tell him I'll take Cory to work with me. Between her grandmother and me, I think she might enjoy the day with us in the shop, rather than in the Crab Shanty." I offered.

Jeanette said she'd be off by 2:00 p.m. to pick her up.

"Kristen, remember Ethan's father has been alerted about Corbin. He knows not only his wife will be with you, but when he finds out his granddaughter will be too, your shop will be watched until it closes."

"Thanks, Jeanette... maybe I can relax and enjoy the day."

Mrs. Chester had been friends with my mother and when asked to help said... she missed working in the shop on occasion when my mom needed her. It reminded me I hadn't talked to my parents for a few days. When it all died down and I had a chance to tell my mother about Mitch... I would. Right now with all that's happened I didn't want them involved. I'd inform them of my trip to New York on Sunday.

Cory was up and eager to go. Jeanette left for work. Cory wanted pancakes from McDonalds. This sounded good and was a real treat for me... not living close to route 50, there were no McDonalds on the way to work or in the town of Claiborne.

We had time. The shop wouldn't open until 10:00 a.m. and it was only 9:00 now. Cory ate with enthusiasm and finished her pancakes. I ate with eagerness and finished my egg McMuffin.

The day passed quickly with a young child to keep us on the move in the shop. She was given specific chores. She greeted customers and also colored a few Thanksgiving pictures for me, like pumpkins and cornucopias of fruit.

Mrs. Chester and I had a long talk about Mitch and Windward Manor.

"Kristen, I never thought his grandmother even existed." She said.

I assured her she did and why Mitch said she'd left his grandfather. Mrs. Chester said, "I've seen pictures of the Savage men and how they resemble one another."

"Yes they do and Mitch looks like them, but even better."

Her words were. "Of course, why would I think you'd say otherwise."

We both laughed.

It had been such a long time ago, when Mrs. Chester would bandage a skinned knee or make me lunch. Ethan and I were always together. She remarked about the good old days, but said she loved Cory and Jeanette. She was glad Ethan found them. I agreed with her. They were fantastic... and special.

Jeanette picked up Cory after we'd had lunch and I was to treat them to dinner. We'd go someplace novel and different, but Ethan had customers... and had to work.

Now, we'd eat at the Crab Shanty.

One more day was all I'd have to wait and I'd be with Mitch. I guess I should call my mother tonight.

I was hesitant, but phoned, mom. There was a lot to tell her. She'd listen and every now and then say *okay, yes,* and let me ramble on and on.

When I finished she said, "So, you met your prince charming. It all sounds romantic, are you sure this is what you want?"

My mother began to aggravate me. I paced at her remarks and interrupted her, "Mom, I can't believe you'd even ask me this question after all the years of dreams and research I've done on Windward Manor. The bonus is, Mitch. I have to say if he wasn't a part of the Savage family or owner of the manor... I'd still have fallen for him. I can't wait for you to meet him. He's special— almost too special."

"That's what I mean, is this too good to be true?" She asked.

Now I was furious, "No... no not at all! Maybe I haven't depicted him correctly. You'll see when you meet him."

"And when, Kristen... might this be?" She replied with annoyance.

I tried to calm myself... but my mother could hear my reaction to her questions.

"I promise we'll work on it." I said with respect.

"Will you move in with him, Kristen?" She queried.

I didn't falter, "Yes."

"What will become of the house?" Was her demand.

"Mom, I haven't gotten that far. I will let you know when the time comes. I'll be in New York next week, but home in time to open the shop... and mom... be happy for me, because I am."

"Okay, I'll tell your father, but keep me informed. You know we love you and want you to be happy."

I shook my head, "Yes, mom. I know. Love you, talk to you later. Bye." I flopped down on the bed exasperated with her attitude. She was not one bit excited for me. Why not? I couldn't figure out why she wouldn't be happy for me... unless after the way things went with Ethan, then Corbin perhaps she didn't want to become excited, possibly she was worried this would be another let down for me.

I calmed myself.

Maybe I overreacted?

Mitch called. He spoke about my being in New York with him and how many hours we had before we'd be together. Our conversation lasted an hour.

He informed me before he hung up, "I'll be up early and in my office to make sure I'm ready by the time you arrive."

Chapter 31

My excitement ran on high. Today was Sunday. All I had to do was get through a few hours of work and I'd be off to meet, Mitch. I couldn't wait to see him. Jeanette would work with me today. Cory would be with her grandmother.

I went downstairs when I'd readied myself for the day. Ethan and Jeanette talked softly. Something was wrong. I wasn't sure—but I wanted to know. They both looked at me with amalgamated concern.

I couldn't help but ask, "What…what's wrong?"

"I don't know how to say this Kris… but Mitch…"

As soon as he said Mitch, I freaked out, "What happened to, him?" I probed.

"Calm down… he's okay…" Answered Ethan.

I began to panic and shout, "He's okay… what happened?"

"Corbin has been arrested." He responded.

"All right, what does this have to do with, Mitch? He's already said, Corbin was wanted for sabotage and more."

"He went after Mitch early this morning… there was a fight and a gun went off…"

I looked for somewhere to sit, what was he going to say and why hadn't I heard from, Mitch. I was in a panic, "Tell me, Ethan… was… he… hurt?"

"Yes, but not seriously." He said.

"What do you mean… not seriously?" I asked with doubt.

"The gun went off, but it's a flesh wound, he said he was fine. But asked if we could put you on a plane this morning, he wants you with him."

"The shop…? People expect it to be open, but I want to be with Mitch." I began to tremble.

Jeanette took hold of my hands, "Calm down, Kristen. Mom and I will take care of the shop. Ethan will take you to the airport." She let go of my hands and spoke softly to continue to compose me. "Why don't you gather all of your luggage? Can you be ready to leave in a half hour?"

I was in a panic and knew they sensed my anxiety.

"Yes, Jeanette, I'll be ready… but are you and Ethan's mom okay with opening the shop?" I asked.

"We have you covered. Go now. Get ready and Ethan will give you the details on the way."

I shook my head yes, but wasn't sure I was prepared for any particulars. Why do I have to be the cause of Mitch's problems? I wanted this so desperately, but it seems to be jinxed. Mitch's business, his head, his now being shot… what was Corbin thinking? I was never important to him. He doesn't like to lose… that's the entire problem.

I gathered my clothes together, which I'd already prepared most of the items for travel, the only thing was, we probably wouldn't go to dinner. I needed to change into a more appropriate yet comfortable outfit.

I changed into a pair of casual, light wool lined slacks of chocolate brown and an embellished black cashmere sweater, with a pair of black heeled boots.

I was dressed, had my garment bag. Ethan went for my suitcase and carry on.

It was cool here today and New York's temperature was ten degrees colder. I'd carry a jacket.

I kissed Jeanette goodbye. "If you have any questions. Call me." I reminded her.

"Kristen, we've got this. My mother-in-law will know what to do. We'll be fine... don't worry." She assured me.

"If you're not busy... close early." I told her.

Ethan had the car loaded. He wasn't driving Mitch's car and he did not allow me to drive either.

"Kristen, you and Mitch can take an airport limo when you return."

Terribly upset and nervous I responded, "Yes, it would be best. I don't know where Mitch has been shot and he probably shouldn't drive."

I was in a daze when Ethan began to tell me Corbin waited for Mitch at his office this morning, there was an argument and then a struggle over the gun when it went off...

"I can't tell you any more than what I was told, because this is all I know and Corbin is in custody."

I looked at Ethan, "Did you talk to, Mitch?"

He looked straight ahead as he drove and answered, "I did."

I was concerned, "Why didn't he call me?" I asked.

Ethan wouldn't look at me, "I don't think he wanted to upset you."

"I don't believe you've told me the entire story. What else?" I probed.

Now Ethan looked at me and said, "I don't know anymore."

When we'd reach the airport, I'd call Mitch to check on him. I wasn't convinced he was okay.

Upon our arrival to BWI, Ethan helped me unload my luggage. He gave me a hug. I checked my suitcase and garment bag outside at the express check-in. He walked away, got into his car and waved good-bye.

This was highly unusual for Ethan.

I was checked in and went to my gate. There was an hour wait. It was early and I'd be in New York by 11:00 a.m. When seated, I retrieved my phone from my carry on and phoned Mitch. It went to voice mail. I left a message and hoped before I boarded the plane I'd hear from him.

No such luck.

Seated on the plane, aware I'd be to Mitch soon… the worry didn't seem to subside. I wasn't one to use my phone on the plane to text him. I had so much on my mind… I placed my head against the window and thought about us.

I wasn't sure what to expect when the plane landed

I found my way to baggage claim and looked around for Mitch. I didn't see him, but saw a young man dressed in a suit and tie with a chauffeur's hat. He held a sign, KSS International Shipping.

I approached him, unsure of why Mitch wasn't in attendance. He asked if I was Kristen Kendal?

I responded nervously, "I expected Mr. Savage."

"I know you did and I'll take you to him. I'm Burns. Show me which luggage is yours."

I pointed as my garment bag and suitcase appeared on the belt. Burns removed the two items and walked with me to the exit, out into the cold, and opened the door on the limousine for me. He placed my luggage in the trunk. I turned my phone on and tried Mitch—only to receive his voice mail… again.

Now the tears began to gather behind my eyes… they'd soon travel down my face. Something was terribly wrong. I was positive Ethan knew, but felt he'd spare me the truth for a few more hours.

The limo driver drove in front of New York-Presbyterian Hospital. I almost lost it and the muffin I'd eaten at the airport.

Burns said, "Ms. Kendal, I'll take your luggage to Mrs. Savage's home. You're to report to the nurse's station on the 4th floor."

He must have noticed a change in the pallor of my face. He reached out his hand to grasp my arm and said, "Mr. Savage will be okay. He's waiting for you."

His kindness was acknowledged, "Thank you, Burns."

The front door to the hospital was entered. An elevator was to take me to the 4th floor. The doors opened into a lobby, a few feet beyond was an information station.

I approached the desk an asked what room Mr. Savage was in.

Before I was able to hear what the nurse was to tell me… a woman, an elegant woman approached me. "Kristine…?"

"Kristen… yes?"

"I'm Mitch's, grandmother."

Sure the shock of seeing her was evident on my face… she

appeared young, but then I remembered she may have only been sixteen or seventeen when her son was born.

"Mitchell, is in surgery. Come sit down."

"In surgery?" I know she could see the astonished look on my face. "I'm sorry I had no idea." The floodgates opened and tears began to pour. "No one told me the truth. Please tell me he's okay... please."

"He will be when he sees you. He made me promise when I made the call to your friend Ethan and made arrangements for your flight, you'd be here when he came out of surgery."

I buried my face in my hands for a moment and let the tears flow. I looked up at a woman who didn't show the least bit of emotion towards me, she seemed detached from my feelings and frame of mind.

I felt inclined to say, "I didn't know how severely he was hurt. I sensed something was wrong when Ethan told me. How critical is he? I feel responsible for all that has happened to him. I didn't know how much I'd love him when we first met. I had no idea."

"You don't know do you?" She asked with contempt.

My facial features had to have changed. I almost lost control. I peered at her in astonishment, "No. I don't know... what's happened to him?" I responded with fear.

She looked at me with malice, "I'm not talking about him. You ruined my life and now you're about to ruin my grandson's."

Confusion set in, "I don't even know you. How can you say... I've ruined your life? I'm sorry if I have in some way. I didn't mean too."

"You're the spitting image of her. The beautiful young woman who captured my husband's heart. He never said, but I watched him gaze upon her portrait... every... single day— until I'd had enough and left. He didn't care about me or the baby I carried. It was you... her... which captivated him like you have now captivated my grandson. If I wouldn't have promised Mitch—I'd send you away!"

My God what was she saying? Where was this portrait? Could it possibly be in the secret room? Was it hidden from her. She said she searched for the hidden room... why was it so important to her? Maybe she wanted to find the portrait and destroy it. Now I was here.... *and to stay with her?*

Would she end the relationship between Mitch and me, like whoever the woman or girl was, who destroyed her love for Mitchell?

I became defensive, "Mrs. Savage, please I've done nothing to you."

She replied, "If I'd known you looked exactly like her even down to your eyes, I wouldn't have made such a promise to Mitch."

She'd no sooner said those words... when the nurse asked if Kristen Kendal was in the waiting room.

"Yes. I'm she."

She said Mitch wanted to see me. He was out of surgery and awake in recovery. I stood and followed her, fully aware his grandmother watched me. I told the nurse I'd no idea what happened and the type of surgery Mitch had been through.

She informed me, "A bullet lodged in his right shoulder very close to the subclavian vein, which supplies blood to his heart."

"I was told it was a flesh wound. I didn't know he was hospitalized and had surgery. I've only arrived a short time ago and was flown in from Maryland." I said with complete ignorance.

"He's asked for you since he came out of the anesthesia... I'm glad you arrived on time."

"So am I... so am I." I repeated.

She showed me into the cubical. I went to him, he sensed I was there, opened his eyes, and reached for my hand. I gave him my left hand. My right hand covered my mouth to hold back the sound which was a tortured—eruption of desperation. Tears began their flow once again.

Between sobs I rambled on, "Mitch, I hadn't an inkling until this minute what happened to you. No one would tell me. I'm sorry, this is all my fault. Nothing good has come from our meeting. Your head, business, being shot, and your grandmother's hate for me."

He squeezed my hand. He wasn't fully awake, and on pain medication, but said softly and honestly, "Love... came from our meeting and don't ever forget... how much I love you."

Chapter 32

I sat in the chair next to his bed, he'd be moved to a room soon. He slept. I didn't know how to appease his grandmother. There was no way possible for me to stay with her. How could I get my things from her house?

I'd have to stay in a hotel. Once Mitch was moved to his room maybe I'd get Burns' phone number and ask him to retrieve my luggage.

The nurse showed me to the visitor's area until Mitch was settled in a room. When I entered the lounge, my luggage was on the floor.

His grandmother said, "I can't let you stay in my home. Here are your things."

I caught a glimpse of Burns and went after him, spoke softly, and asked him to take my things to Mitch's.

He said, "I was told not to take you there."

"By whom?" I asked.

He whispered softy, "By Mrs. Savage."

"Burns, I need your phone number. I'll explain. Please take my call when she's not around."

He looked at me. I gave a silent plea. He slid me his card

so she wouldn't see and left. I told him he'd hear from me later. Seated next to my luggage until told Mitch was in his room... there would be no conversation with his grandmother on my part.

Mrs. Savage approached me and said, "I held up my end of the promise. He saw you... now you may leave."

I stood my ground and said, "No."

She went in front of me and told the nurse I was not to see Mitch. The nurse said he was wide awake and asked for me. I picked up my baggage and followed the nurse and Mrs. Savage.

Mitch was in a reclined position in bed. He watched me carry my suitcases. There was a look of dismay on his face.

His facial features read he was upset. "Gran, what's the problem. Kristen's luggage was to be taken to your house?"

"I don't want her there or near you. I want her to go... now!"

My luggage was placed in a corner. I moved to his bed. "Mitch, I'll be fine. There is no need to discuss this now."

I'd seen him upset before and knew he was irritated, "Yes there is... what's going on... Gran?"

"Mitch... please, rest. I'm here and I won't leave. I'll be here when you wake." I placated.

He reached for my hand, "No. I want to know, Kristen?"

He looked at his grandmother. She began to speak, "She's the one who ruined my life with your grandfather. He gazed at her portrait every day. He hid it in the secret room. I know he did. That's why I left him... he was in love with her."

And she pointed to me.

Mitch tried to stay calm, "Grandmother... listen to yourself. Kristen wasn't around when you were married to my grandfather."

"It's her, the same grey eyes, the long beautiful raven hair.

I saw the portrait. She was beautiful and he loved her... not me!" She screamed.

For what he'd been through, Mitch sounded composed, "Grandmother, sit down. I know how distraught you've been since I was injured. I'll have them give you a sedative and Burns will take you home. You need to rest."

The nurse entered the room with medication to be injected into Mitch's IV. He asked her to call Dr. Stevens for his grandmother, he thought she needed to be seen. His fear was the shock of his surgery was too much on her.

The nurse responded, "I'll be sure Dr. Stevens is paged."

Mitch told her, "Before you give me any medication I want Burns in here." He asked for his phone. I took it from his effects on the table next to the bed.

"Burns' number is on speed dial number two." He stated.

I pushed the two and the phone began to ring. I pushed the speaker button and watched Mitch focus on what he needed to do for his grandmother's welfare... even though he was in pain.

I heard Burns answer. Mitch asked him to come to his room. Burns relayed he'd be right there. He must have waited to take Mrs. Savage home.

Dr. Stevens appeared. Mitch told him what he thought his grandma was going through because she'd been talking nonsense and he was sure she could use a sedative and sleep.

"Mrs. Savage, come with me. I'd like to check your heart and blood pressure this has been a very wearisome day for you. Mitch will be fine. He's okay."

She got up to leave and said, "Mitch, I don't want... Caroline, here."

Firmly he said, "Gran, this is, Kristen... and she will stay."

His grandmother was taken from the room and I watched

as the medication being given would allow Mitch to rest. He told the nurse, "Please bring a chair which reclines. Kristen will spend the night."

She left the room. I leaned over to kiss him. He was groggy, but was able to understand when I said, "I'm here, Mitch. Please rest. We'll talk later."

It was a long day. I watched him sleep. Ethan called to check on me.

"I'd never expected to find Mitch in such a state and the surgery he's been through," I said.

Ethan stated, "I'm sorry, but I didn't have the heart to tell you the truth and have you worry until you reached New York."

I thanked him for his thoughtfulness and told him soon I'd bring Mitch back to Windward Manor.

All day and night they gave Mitch antibiotics and pain meds continually through his IV. He had a slight temperature. I tried to make sure when he was lucid, he drank fluids.

The day seemed to never end and night was even longer as he'd call out in his sleep for me. Each time he did I'd rise out of the sleep chair and come to his side. His left shoulder, chest and around his back were bandaged.

I couldn't believe Corbin did this to him and I couldn't believe what Mitch's grandmother said. This was part of the mystery we needed to solve. She vanished. Some thought she'd drown and others thought Mitch's grandfather killed her.

I think once we were able to explore the hidden room we'd

soon find the secret and decipher the unknown. But for now all I wanted was for Mitch to get well.

I was sorry his grandmother needed help. I felt badly she'd sustain such a shock, her memory took her back to a time in her life where it left a deep impression and scar on her recollection.

No wonder she never remarried, she was young and couldn't understand how she carried the child of a man who didn't love her. Things of this nature were viewed differently... the humiliation must have been more than she could endure.

Chapter 33

T he week passed slowly. Mitch was far from better. The
staples, and sutures were removed from his head, and the
drain removed from his shoulder. Bandaged again he moaned
when he was moved. I couldn't hold back the tears.

"Kristen, I'm okay. Please don't cry." He said.

"I blame myself for all your troubles. It hurts me to know
you hurt."

I'd move to him when the nurse would leave. "Mitch, do
you honestly think this will work between us? No one knows
what happened between Caroline and your grandfather. He died
by himself and your grandmother has been scarred for life. I
couldn't stand the thought of you suffering the rest of your life
because of me."

"Kristen, you are not Caroline." He said affirmably.

I became annoyed, "I know I'm not. But why is she saying
I look like her and what happened between them." I questioned.

Those blue eyes searched mine and he spoke calmly, "When
we go home we'll find the answers we need. Come closer. I
want to kiss you."

I leaned closer to kiss his sensual lips. I'd always want to
feel this way about him.

It was Friday. I should be headed back to Maryland. I couldn't ask friends to continue to open and close my store, it wasn't fair to them. I'd told Brittany and Katie to seek other jobs since the shop wasn't busy enough for me to keep them on... now it had become a problem.

I'd ask Ethan to hang a **closed** sign on the door, until my return.

Mitch was somewhat better and would be released Monday, but he wasn't exactly ready for a flight, or the long drive to Maryland.

While he slept, I took a moment to call my mother. I told her what happened with Corbin and Mitch. I didn't actually know the entire story... I could only relay what I'd heard.

My mother was shocked and couldn't believe what I'd said. She didn't know I was in New York with Mitch and of course when she realized I was, she wanted to know what was to transpire at the shop.

"Mom, last weekend Ethan's mom and his wife Jeanette managed the shop on Sunday. I thought I'd be home by now, but I can't leave Mitch."

"What do you intend to do, Kristen? You still have responsibilities and bills to pay, you just can't ignore them." She voiced.

"Mom, I'm okay monetarily. I have money. I hate to ask for help again this weekend. I'm not sure how soon Mitch can travel."

My mother acted snooty. "Doesn't he have family?"

"His grandmother, but..."

Now she was provoked, "But what, Kristen, she can't take care of him?"

"No. That's not it. It's a long story. It has to do with Windward Manor's mystery."

"Kristen..."

I sensed by my mother's tone she didn't want to hear about Windward Manor or anything related to it.

I became firm, "Mom, Mitch's grandmother isn't well and she can't take care of him right now and he can't travel. If you and dad want to take a trip you could stay at my place. You'd see what I've done to the house... and I know Mrs. Chester would help you in the shop... otherwise, I have to hang a closed sign on the door this weekend and next."

Her voice became brash and she said, "Kristen, you can't do this. Tourists come to the bay town to look in the unique shops, walk the streets and view the quaint city. Thanksgiving is right around the corner then Christmas, you should have your holiday inventory in and set for sale."

"Mom... I know. It's all on order and will be in this week, but I intended it for next weekend... I'm not sure if I will be home by then."

I heard Mitch say, "Tell your mother we'll be home this week. I don't want her upset with either of us."

I turned to see he was awake and placed my hand over the mouth piece on the phone. "Mitch, you can't travel." I responded.

"Kristen, I can and we will." He was being firm, but pleasant.

"I heard him, Kristen, he's right and this isn't a good time for us to leave Arizona, it's cold in Maryland this time of year."

"Okay, mom. I'll talk with you later."

I ended my call.

I turned to look at him. I'd stood by the window with hope I wouldn't wake him.

"I'm sorry I woke you."

I walked to him and his response was, "Between Corbin,

my grandmother, and your mother... do you think we'll ever get this romance off the ground?"

I knew how he felt, "I sure hope so." It was said miserably. By now I stood next to him and held his hand.

"When they release me, I'll rent a stretch limo and we're going to Maryland. I want to be with you in our home, and find out what the hell this mystery is about and put it to sleep."

"You shouldn't travel, Mitch." It was said with concern.

"And you shouldn't have had to sleep in a chair all week. I've never seen my grandmother act like this in all my years." He said sympathetically.

I looked at him seriously and softly said with compassion, "Mitch... she was deeply marked from her experience as a young girl... I can't blame her."

"Kristen, time has passed. I can give her sympathy because I love her, but she has carried this too far for me. She has to get a grip on it and herself. She's an educated woman, raised my father, and me. She's not a dumb woman by any means and why she insists you're Caroline is beyond me." He shook his head in disbelief, "I know she said you look like her, but even if you do... you're not Caroline... and I'm not my grandfather." He paused out of exasperation. "Can you see if Jeanette or Ethan's mom will handle the shop this weekend, and we'll be home by Monday or Tuesday?"

"Mitch... I want you home. I need you with me. I wish for us to live in your house, but I don't want you to hurt on the trip home." I appealed.

Now he smiled, "I'll have Burns fix the inside of the limo and make it like a bed, we can both sleep on the ride."

After sleeping in a chair, it sounded perfect to me.

Chapter 34

Mitch was released from the hospital. Mrs. Chester took care of the shop, and we were on our way to Maryland.

He decided it would be easy to work from the house instead of New York.

His grandmother was upset with him. He told her if she wanted to see him before his return to New York in a few weeks, she'd have to come to him.

Mitch would set up his office in Windward Manor, and I'd open my shop only on weekends until Christmas. From Christmas to the first of May the shop would be closed and we'd planned to travel.

He was right. Burns fixed the back of the limo and it was quite comfortable. Now his shoulder only sported a small bandage, but was in a sling. He was to use his arm on occasion… like very little.

Mitch took his pain medication and slept once we were settled to travel. The limo was more comfortable than the sleep chair I'd spent so much time in and I fell asleep easily.

Eventually Burns needed to make a pit stop for me. By the time I was back in the limo Mitch was awake. And in good spirits.

"You know... this reminds me of the night we slept in your hallway, it's quite cozy for travel. I think I'm hungry." He grinned when he yelled to be heard, "What do you say Burns... can you find us a place to eat?"

"Will you be okay to get in and out of the limo?" I asked.

His smile said he felt better, "I think I can. Might need your help. Like a kiss for encouragement."

My grin said, I was all for it.

The three of us ate lunch, were back in the limousine, and knew neither of us would sleep again. There was only two hours left in the trip. The rig... which was set up for our travels was folded, and left plenty room to sit.

It was time for Mitch to tell me what happened with Corbin. Why he was shot. I understood Burns was also his bodyguard and wondered where he'd been when the shot was fired.

Mitch began his explanation.

"Burns dropped me off at the office exceptionally early so I'd have in a full day before we'd pick you up at 8:00 p.m. What I didn't realize when he went for coffee... Corbin was lying in wait for me. We had words and Corbin pulled out a gun. The move completely shocked me. I'd no idea he'd go so far." I saw Mitch became disturbed, but continued, "He'd been a good employee for five years and I never expected this from him. Burns returned with coffee and startled Corbin. I made an attempt to remove the gun from his hand and in the scuffle the gun went off. It was my own damn fault the bullet caught me. I should have punched, Corbin in the face and taken the gun from him."

"Mitch, I'm so sorry. I had no idea he'd act this way. He didn't show his true colors until we were engaged the second year. Then he became dictatorial and I found he cheated on me. I wouldn't accept this in my life and considered my return to Maryland when my parents offered me the gift of their home and my mother's shop."

"So, if I become bossy, you'll leave me." Now he smiled.

"Only if you cheat on me... it's so demoralizing." I replied.

He pulled me close to him. His good arm wrapped around my shoulder. "I'll never cheat on you. You are my world now and always will be. I love you and I've said we will live in my home and you've never said no, but do you know it means I want to marry you and spend the rest of my life with you."

My eye contact with him became blurry, "I wasn't sure but I hoped... it's what you meant."

He removed his good arm from around my shoulder and gently kissed my lips.

"You know I had big plans for us this past week, dinners out, walks around New York and all you saw was the inside of a hospital room."

He reached into his pocket and removed a small velvet jeweler's box. "I had the perfect evening planned for you and me, but it never happened and I don't want to wait any longer to give this to you." He said.

The box was opened with one hand and he asked again, "Will you marry me, Kristen. I give you my heart for the rest of my life."

I knew what my answer was since I'd first laid eyes on him, "Yes, Mitch. I've loved you since the first time I saw you... you didn't much like me then, but I knew I'd never love another."

My hands were gently placed upon his face and drawn to me. I wanted to feel his mouth on mine and the kiss which followed was positively breathtaking.

He removed the ring with his right hand, let the box drop and reached for my left hand. When he slid the exquisite diamond on my finger, it felt right. I had no reservations about him or his love for me. It was so different than when Corbin proposed, I'd had uncertainties at the time and they came full circle.

"Mitch... this ring and you are so much more than I ever thought would be in my life. It's beautiful... I love it... and you."

Chapter 35

W e neared the town of Claiborne. Mitch asked if I thought until we shopped for food and moved my possessions, we should stay at my place tonight. It sounded logical.

"Kristen, I want to take time to get you settled in our home. I also want to stock the kitchen, find out when the chef will arrive, and search through the secret room."

"Sounds like we'll be busy, but it also sounds like fun. I can't wait to setup house with you. I think the kitchen could use some organization. The dishes and small appliances need to be put away." I said.

He smiled, "We may leave it to the chef, so he can find the things he needs. By the way have you thought about what you will do with your house?"

He watched me closely, "Mitch, we could sell or rent it. Where will, Burns live?" I asked.

"For now he'll stay at the Hampton Inn. I think I'm safe, since Corbin has been arrested." He replied.

"What will they do with him?" I asked.

"I really don't know. He has a few charges against him, illegal weapon, intent to kill or maim, sabotage and I think a few more charges. Do you feel sorry for him?" He inquired with apprehension.

"No, Mitch. I needed to make sure you were safe. I couldn't

stand if something should happen to you. I can't seem to get past the fact you're hurt now… and it's my fault. I'm so sorry." I said.

"Kristen, don't let me hear you say those words again, it's not your fault. I found he's embezzled from my company. He knew I was aware of it and didn't want me to tell anyone. His thoughts were to get rid of me, and whoever took over wouldn't find out. The sabotage came later after we met. Corbin, knew I wanted us to be together."

Burns must have had my address because before I knew it, we were on the crushed oyster shell lane.

"Mitch, would Burns want to live here?" I inquired.

"You know—I don't know? I guess we'll have to ask him."

It was still light outside and the view of the bay and the bridge looked imposing.

Burns held the door and we climbed from the limo. "Wow, this is quite impressive. All this water and land, a lot different from where I grew up" He said.

We stood outside the car for a minute… Burns was asked a few questions.

"What do you think? Would you like to live in this town, on the water or go back to New York?"

"Do I have a choice, Mr. Savage?" He asked.

"Yes, you can live in this house when I have Ms. Kendal situated in our home, you can be near if I need you, or go back to New York until I need you. How about tomorrow you be here by noon and take a look inside the house, see what you think?"

"Sounds like a plan to me. Is there good fishing from the pier?"

I answered him, "Burns, there's great fishing and crabbing from the pier."

"I've never eaten crabs, seen them, but never tasted them. I know Marylander's have a way with steaming and seasoning, but that's all I know."

I told him we'd see if Ethan had crabs for tomorrow evening, we'd go to the Crab Shanty, and he could see the town. Then he could decide.

Mitch told him there was a college nearby, if he wanted to go during the day, he wouldn't be needed days unless he had to be in New York.

Burns smiled, "You know it might be nice here, less hustle and more time for things I'd like to see and do."

He unloaded our luggage and carried it into the house, "Nice place. I could get into this. Never had a lot of grass around where I came from, mostly concrete… this is different… pleasant."

"Well it's here or next door in the last wing on the house, where the restorations aren't quite complete." Mitch added.

"Might be too weird. I've heard you talk about… ghosts." He replied.

"You will have to figure it out for yourself, Burns. You can keep your same salary if you stay here, but may need to be called upon to help with a few chores, or take a reduction in salary and head back to New York and get paid when I'd need you."

Burns had a huge grin on his face, "Well I guess you just made up my mind. Not a thing in New York I'll miss."

I'm sure Burns or whatever his first name was would fit in Claiborne. He was a nice looking young man about twenty-three. We had a few young ladies, who'd be glad to make his acquaintance.

He was tall, quite muscular, and if he was a bodyguard he'd had some police training. We'd take him into the Crab Shanty and I guarantee he'd find himself feeling special. He seemed very nice and did say he'd like to take a course in criminal justice if it was offered at the college. We could introduce him to Ethan's father, our chief of police.

It was late enough, Mitch and I felt we could eat again. There wasn't much in the house. I thought an omelet would work. I had onions and cheese for the omelet, bread was in the freezer for toast. I took a can of frozen orange juice from the freezer and we soon had a meal.

Burns was to stay at the Hampton Inn and I'm sure he found a place to eat. We didn't ask him to stay because I needed to do laundry and was in my robe, Mitch was in his robe... although it was a major feat to put his arm through the sleeve.

We became engrossed with our to do list for tomorrow... and time got away from us. We'd definitely be here a few more days before we'd settle in Windward Manor.

I needed to pack up my belongings and the manor needed to have the kitchen stocked with food.

Mitch was tired, it had been a long day for him. He hadn't asked for his pain medication all day, but I could see he was in need of it.

We'd gone upstairs to bed.

I touched his good arm gently, "Mitch, I think you need your pain meds."

He looked at me lovingly and said, "Yes... you're right. I

wanted to spend this time with you. If I'd taken it earlier I'd have gone to bed without you. I've missed you this past week. I'm beginning to think I'll never have the chance to make love to you. I've never had so many injuries in my life. I hope I'm past them now. Do you think Jeanette can take a look at the wound and dress it for me?"

I was sure she wouldn't mind.

We were preparing to climb into bed and I answered, "I'll call her tomorrow, maybe she can stop after work. I'll let Burns pick-up gauze pads and tape. Let me help you out of your robe. It's still cool in here. Will you be okay without a shirt? I shouldn't have turned the heat back so far when I left. Can I snuggle against you to stay warm?"

"I love you Kristen, and I'm so glad I've found you." He said with affection.

"I love you too. Get some sleep. It's been a long week for both of us." I replied

"Yes, I've missed the feel of you." Was his reply.

He was settled in bed, had his medication, I couldn't wait to get under the covers, and move my body close to him. His kisses always set my soul on fire.

I couldn't wait for what was to come next.

Chapter 36

I opened my eyes to a room full of sunshine. We'd slept in the guest room last night and Kristen forgot to pull the shade. It looked like an ideal day. After all the trouble I'd been through lately... I hoped the day turned out to be perfect. The way the morning appeared... it should be beautiful.

Kristen was asleep. I didn't want to wake her, she'd had a rough week in New York, between my grandmother and me. I never thought I'd love someone so much and to know she loves me was even better.

I realized how much I loved her when Corbin purposely wanted to keep me in New York, and rushed here to make sure she was unharmed, and saw how terrified she was when she arrived in New York to find I'd had surgery. Then I knew for sure... she truly felt the same way about me.

She looked peaceful sleeping. Her long raven hair was spilled across the whiteness of the pillowcase. I couldn't wait for my shoulder to heal to take her in both my arms, wrap her silky hair around my hand and drag her sexy mouth to mine. She was beautiful. I knew thoughts of this nature would land me into trouble, because I couldn't do a thing about it.

Unfortunately, I needed to eat before my pain medication. After a night of sleep my shoulder was stiff and sore. I tried yesterday to move it slightly and would try more today, but I could use the help of the drug.

I slid out of bed and tried not to wake Kristen. I thought if I showered, I might feel better and erase the thoughts I had of wanting her. I knew it would be hard to do, because the longer I gazed upon her... the more I desired her.

I didn't hear the shower water, but Mitch wasn't in bed... then he opened the bathroom door, was in pain, and in need of his medication. He came towards me with his lean hard body, droplets of water coursing off his chest, which was slightly furry, and rippled with muscle down to a ridged abdomen. His hair wet and uncombed. The sexy shadow of a dark overnight growth on his face made his blue eyes seem even bluer... with a towel wrapped around his waist, he was definitely the sexiest man I'd ever seen.

"Mitch, I'm sorry I overslept... you need your medication."

He grabbed a second towel and dried the portion of his upper body not bandaged. He walked closer to me.

"I didn't want to wake you, I'm sorry." He whispered.

Heat washed through me and my stomach muscles clenched as the corner of his sexy mouth edged upwards. I saw the hunger in his eyes. I knew he felt the same thing I did.

He sat on the side of the bed and touched my face tenderly, "You're beautiful...even while you sleep. I want to hold you with both arms and kiss your sexy mouth. It frustrates me to know I have to wait longer to make love to you."

I sat up and wrapped my arms around his neck, careful not to touch his shoulder. H pulled my face to his for a scorching kiss, one so intoxicating I wasn't sure I could think straight. I'd never been kissed this way before… I didn't want it to end… but knew it had to. A few more days… and I'd count the minutes.

His look of love… left me stirred with desire.

"I love you, Mitch…"

"I know, baby. Soon I'll be better. I start therapy tomorrow and the sutures can be removed. I promise you… it will be worth the wait."

I kissed him this time, then got out of bed, and reached for my robe. "I'll start the coffee and breakfast… come downstairs when you're ready."

It was a beautiful morning, but I wanted more of Mitch. He was right it would happen soon enough, but seemed almost impossible. I never felt this way about Corbin. These were new, raw emotions, and different than I've ever experienced.

He came down the stairs. His hair was damp and tousled. His jeans rode low on his hard body and took my breath. He carried a lightweight, chocolate brown V-neck sweater and his sling… and asked if I could help him.

Before my words could form an answer… I walked close to him, positioned my arms around his waist, and my head on his chest. Light kisses were placed there… then his mouth. A look of satisfaction was written on his face. The sweater was taken from him.

"I'm not sure I want you to stop." He blurted.

"Trust me—I don't want to… medically I don't think it's wise."

His sigh and expression showed… *frustration.*

He was helped with his sweater. I didn't have to move his

shoulder, but gently his arm was moved into position until put into the sling.

Breakfast was almost ready. Coffee was hot. When he sat, a cup was placed in front of him. "I hope you like French toast? The bread had been frozen. When it's less than fresh, it makes the best toast." I told him.

His eyes never left my face. His smile said he'd like whatever I made, "Sounds great."

"Mitch, how about after breakfast we take a walk along the beach from my house to yours? From the kitchen window the bay looks smooth... like glass today."

He replied, "How about... from this cottage... to our home?"

Chapter 37

W e took our jackets and made our way from my home to the manor. Burns, was to stop by today to look over the house to see if he'd definitely stay in Claiborne.

I came to a standstill and so did Mitch, his facial expression showed curiosity about what was on my mind and why we were stopped.

With careful thought the question was approached, "I think if Burns lives in my cottage and we are to be married… should the cottage become a part of Windward Manor again?"

Mitch looked thoughtful and readily gave his answer, "In conversation only. I don't feel after the way your mother thought of our relationship—she'd be happy if you sold the home given to you. I'll pay you rent for Burns to reside there. It will go into your personal account. There is no way we want your mother to think I'd take advantage of you. Your shop, your money. But when we do anything or purchase something you may want… I'll take care of you. I want to be a real husband and support you from your sexy underwear to our fantastic trips and whatnot … all to be paid by me."

We enjoyed our walk, but didn't enter the manor. We came back to the cottage hand in hand to wait for Burns.

Mitch wanted to know Burns' thoughts on being a resident of Claiborne and continuing to work for him. This told me he was serious about his company being run from here. I was pleased with the belief all would work out well for us and I could continue with my shop, but wanted someone reliable to cover for me... when needed.

Burns arrived by noon. I heard him approach the steps to the front door. Mitch opened the door to greet him. By the time I'd finished my presentation of the house and grounds... he was sold on his stay in Claiborne.

I'd already made a call to Ethan about crabs tonight and we were in luck. He'd received a shipment and there were some jumbos among them. Plus... he'd been asked to stay open and serve a full menu, which included the best crabs.

We were set for 6:00 p.m.

"Burns, how would you like to meet the chief of police... if you want to pursue the town's police force part-time." He responded with a smile until he saw Mitch's expression.

I wasn't sure Mitch was too thrilled about the loss of his bodyguard and driver, but with Mitch here... Burns wouldn't be needed often. Claiborne was in no way like New York City.

"We'll eat crabs tonight, Burns. I know you'll enjoy them. Mitch will too, but I'll have to pick his."

His shoulder wouldn't allow him the movement he needed to fend for himself with the eating of crabs.

A few errands were given to Burns.

"Burns, will you pick up a few things from Walmart for me. I need boxes and tape to finish packing."

Of course he said yes.

"You do know your help will be necessary to carry my items next door. I also require bandages and other supplies for Mitch's shoulder."

"Not a problem, got it covered." He responded.

He left to pick up the few items asked for.

Upon his return I inquired. "What would you guys like to eat for lunch before we go to the Crab Shanty? Will Chinese work?"

A response of, "Yes." Was heard.

I settled Mitch on the sofa in the living room with the TV controller and set about packing up my possessions. Burns carried each box to the limo.

Our meal was delivered. We ate and I continued to pack.

The day got away from me. Before I knew it, it was time to shower and change for dinner.

When we arrived at the Shanty. The place was packed. I saw Katie among the crowd… she waved.

I waved a hello, and caught her out of the corner of my eye… she stared at the new man in town.

Her eyes followed him to our table.

Ethan brought out steamed, fat crabs. They were hot.

Burns was excited. He turned his head to glance at Katie… and then the crabs. He smiled and said, "You know boss, I think I'm gonna like it here."

Mitch and I both laughed.

The crabs were great. Ethan joined us—to talk. "How you feeling, Mitch?" he asked. "I didn't like Corbin when Kristen was forced to introduce me." He said. "By the way Jeanette will be by tomorrow to take a look at your shoulder. Got to get back to my kitchen. Good to see you two and glad to have you home."

"Thanks, Ethan." We said.

Katie came to the table, her parents left. "What's happening at the shop, Kristen? I haven't seen you around."

I tried to explain about Windward Manor, Mitch, Burns, and what happened with Corbin.

I asked her to join us. Her eyes lit up, "Katie, allow me to introduce you. Alan Burns… and my fiancé, Mitch Savage."

"Very nice to meet you. I was worried what may have happened to you, Kris… since I hadn't seen you around. I began to wonder… If something awful had occurred. I knew the day you and Brittany told me about Corbin… I didn't like him."

She began unconsciously to help Burns with his crabs. We discussed possibly her help in the shop again. She seemed interested. By now she and Burns were entertained with one another and immersed in conversation.

I sensed Mitch was tired and was pleased Ethan made him a crab cake… I couldn't pick fast enough to fill him. At least he had enough in his stomach to take the last dose of medicine for the night.

We came in Mitch's car to the Shanty. The limo was filled with boxes. Burns was to return later to the hotel with Mitch's car and arrive tomorrow to help move more boxes.

I asked, "Burns, are you ready to leave? We'll take the uneaten portion of crabs with us. You can finish them tomorrow."

Katie volunteered to drive him to my house when he finished eating.

"If you're sure you don't mind, Katie. You two finish the rest of the crabs. I'm done for the night. Burns, we'll see you about noon again tomorrow, is that good for you... you have the extra key to the car... right?"

"I do in my pocket." He responded.

"Okay, then Mitch and I are set. You take the car, no need to check in with us when Katie brings you to the cottage."

I knew Mitch was in pain... he became quiet.

"Thanks for the crabs. They're great. I'll grab the car, head to the hotel for the night, and be at your house by noon." Burns said.

Mitch finally spoke up and with a smile said. "Be careful with my car, Burns. See you tomorrow."

"You've got it, Mr. Savage." Was heard.

Chapter 38

Mitch was much improved. It had been a long week of preparations for our move. Tomorrow we'd be permanently moved into the manor. The only room in my house, which needed the décor changed was my bedroom. It needed Burns' touch.

He wasn't into the pink coverlet and the other frills in the room. It now held his personal signature. He'd changed the pictures and comforter.

Burns moved most of my boxes into the manor last week and then headed back to New York for his possessions.

He returned the rented limo in New York. The company supplied him with a Mercedes sedan when Mitch would need him, for his travels.

Mitch and I hadn't begun to search the secret room, while in the process of the move. Between my possessions, the chef's arrival, kitchen arrangement, purchase of food, and other supplies—we'd been busy.

Mitch wasn't allowed to do much of what he wanted… because I wouldn't let him.

Our last night in my house, and each night since we'd been home, the soft glow of light remained in the window of Windward Manor. Now the house was prepared to accept Mitch and me… we'd have time to find out what all the mystery was about.

Mitch had very few phone conversations with his grandmother. She wouldn't concede in her opinion of me and he tried his best to be nice to her. I sensed his patience was about to wear thin and wasn't sure what we'd find in the secret room, but no matter what it was… I didn't think it would help—but only hinder the situation between them—*and possibly between us.*

Our last night in my home was to be a memory. Mitch's shoulder felt better and when he pulled me into his arms… I knew the wait was over.

We headed to bed. Mitch's good arm wrapped across my shoulders. I turned to look at him, and gently touched his cheek. I felt the smooth shadow of facial hair.

His gaze told me of our night together. He brushed his lips against mine. A kiss which said a thousand times he loved me. At the top of the stairs the need we felt turned into a passion of want and release.

Mitch became serious, his voice a whisper, "I've waited for this moment ever since our night in your hallway to protect us from the storm. It seems I've waited forever to wrap my hands in those glossy strands of your silky… raven hair."

I pulled her head back to look into her eyes and my mouth crushed down on hers. Heat burned through me, a warmth I'd never felt before, but with the same persistent need which had grown even more powerful than the first time I saw her.

Her light touch and commanding kisses to my shoulder and chest told me she felt the same way. She'd be mine always... after this night.

We'd gotten a late start this morning after our night of lovemaking. I felt replete and at ease with each and every touch from Mitch's love. We both looked forward to residing in the manor and a dinner to be served in the gracious dining room.

Our chef... Paul Sebastian, came highly recommended. We'll see what Mitch's thoughts are when the meal was over. Paul was to prepare a special dinner tonight.

He wouldn't be a live in chef, didn't live far from the town of Claiborne, and had a family of his own. His qualifications had been referred through close friends of Mitch's.

With the knowledge I liked to cook and so did Mitch, we'd handle breakfast, lunch, and dinners on weekends, unless we were to have company, but Paul's nightly meals would be a time for us to relax and enjoy our new life together.

Dinner tonight was to be special. It would be our first night in Windward Manor... as a couple... to plan our wedding. We counted on the weather to be warm for a May ceremony. With Thanksgiving around the corner then Christmas we had a little over six months to make sure our ceremony would be flawless.

It had to be picture-perfect. Every feeling I had for Mitch was more than perfect. After our first meeting and his heartlessness towards me, I couldn't believe I was here now— as we prepared for our lives together.

Before we left my cottage we'd had breakfast and looked forward to begin our search through the books and ledgers behind the secret door. Not sure of what we'd find, the excitement of Mitch, dinner, our move, and our search— overwhelmed me.

To find out the mystery would allow us to complete renovations in the far wing for guests. It was a slight possibility the work wouldn't be finished until we knew why the light would glow each night and why Mitch's grandmother thought I was someone other than who I was.

Chapter 39

Dinner was exactly what the doctor ordered. Delicious, quiet and wonderful. Paul worked wonders with the stuffed rockfish. I remembered the taste of rockfish very well, but hadn't indulged in years. My Dad would catch them to sell at market, and bring home a few. He had his own way to season and bake the fish. They were always enjoyable…but I think Paul's had an edge over my dad's with the crabmeat stuffing.

When we finished dinner, Mitch looked at me and said, "I think Paul will work out just fine. We may use him more often than not."

I smiled. "I guess we won't bump into one another in the kitchen after all."

We laughed, and kissed by the end of the declaration.

The living room or ballroom was too formal to watch TV and relax. Mitch turned the study into our retreat. His desk was at one end of the room closer to the library shelves, which held many first edition books.

The leather-bound volumes were numerous and the scent from the leather, after years, continued to exist within the room.

The other end of the chamber held a very comfortable, soft

leather sofa, two comfortable chairs, coffee table and a wide screen TV. The way the windows were situated in the room gave us a great view of the bay. The flat screen fit quite nicely between a group of them.

This is where we retired… after our meal.

I held my first after dinner brandy snifter with excellent brandy. After all my dreams about Windward Manor over the years… here I sat and enjoyed the company of my fiancé.

Paul and his crew cleaned up our meal and the kitchen. He took time to setup for breakfast. I saw the harvest table was prepared attractively. We'd cook in our new kitchen tomorrow. Eggs Benedict was to be on the menu. Mitch and I'd work together to make it just right.

We sipped on brandy, the television was turned down low and Mitch asked, "Do you think tomorrow will be a good day to start our search in the secret room?"

"I'm aware we need to solve this mystery and tomorrow is good. It doesn't get any better." I replied.

Mitch decidedly had contractors lined up to work in the left wing of the house.

Since Corbin was held without bond, KSS was back on track and Mitch would continue to be off for a few more weeks. Important issues which would arise would be handled from here.

I was beyond happy and couldn't find words to describe the emotions Mitch evoked in me when he sat so near. I may have been sipping on my brandy, but my mind was in many different places and each of those places was with him.

I detected his blue eyes in observance of me— with interest. His look was so intense it was actually felt.

My head turned and my grey eyes glimpsed his way.

"Where are your thoughts? I can see you're off in a cloud, Kristen."

I laughed, "You know me so well." I leaned into him and searched his face. His smile held me captive. I slowly raised my hand to touch him. "They are all thoughts of you and how happy I am."

"I'm happy too. And I think the house maybe, also. There have not been any displays of temper since we've been home. I think its secret wants to be known. Tomorrow we'll begin our search. But tonight my love I have other things on my mind."

I kissed him softly, "I want the same things too."

He removed the brandy snifter from my hand and walked it into the kitchen along with his and checked the new security system. I rose from the sofa. We met in the hallway. I was drawn into his arms and kissed deeply. The hold on one another was firmly and we made our way to the stairs, through the wide hallway.

Once in our bedroom, Mitch assisted me out of my dress. I helped him shed his clothes. His body was 'ripped' my hands on his chest placing soft kisses on his shoulder, released a welcome sound from his lips.

He found my mouth… I whispered his name.

This would be our first night in Windward Manor… and would be magnificent like our last night… in the cottage.

Chapter 40

T he way the master suite was situated, French doors led onto a balcony, which overlooked the bay. I felt gentle morning kisses and realized the drapes had been opened by Mitch to reveal the gleam of sunlight off the water. It was later than I wanted to sleep.

Did we sleep?

He was showered, dressed and ready for the day.

"Good morning my raven haired beauty. I love to watch you sleep... but as I begin to prepare our breakfast, you can either lie here until I call you, take your shower, or come to breakfast in your robe."

I reached up and wrapped my arms around his neck and pulled him closer. "I think I would have preferred your company for a while longer this morning."

"Really, I think you'll be surprised to know it's almost noon." Was his reply.

I couldn't imagine it was so late. I jumped out of bed, "Why did you allow me to sleep this long, I'm going to grow lazy."

"Never my love. Our nights seem to turn to day... and I like it. I can't get enough of you... and anyway I've been up..." He looked at his watch, "All of about a half hour. We'll eventually get more sleep once we collapse from lack of."

We both laughed. He kissed me soundly, and was probably right, but it was now time for me to be out of bed.

I was showered, dressed, and breakfast was ready. Mitch is a great cook. I don't think I could have done any better myself. We sat at the harvest table together, with fresh squeezed orange juice, coffee, and perfect eggs benedict.

"Are you sure we need, Paul? You've made a wonderful meal."

His smile told me he liked my compliment, but so far everything Mitch did... was better than impeccable.

We began our morning off with a walk to the bay, of course we needed our heavier jackets. November was cold and damp, but the sun felt delightful. We walked hand in hand and Mitch laid out our plans for the day.

During the walk a decision was made to host Thanksgiving dinner at our home. Of course he'd invite his grandmother, but we didn't think she'd accept the invitation.

My parents, would probably do the same, but Alex, Ava, Mr. and Mrs. North along with Mr. and Mrs. Chester, Ethan, Jeanette, Cory, and of course Burns. We knew they'd all be here.

It would be arranged.

Our afternoon was to take us into the secret room and find answers. I wanted to know... then again I didn't. I became apprehensive about what we may find and could perhaps drive us apart.

We returned through the back French doors. The fireplace in the study filled the room with warmth. It was pleasant and I trusted it would transfer heat through the stone walls of the secret room.

Mitch looked at me for confirmation this was what needed

to be done. The thought and anticipation of the search had me feeling overcome with nausea. I was warm, but not from the hearth. My hands felt moist. Mitch came to hold me close to his chest.

"Kristen, I haven't seen you this fearful since you found out I'd been shot. Nothing in this house has ever troubled you before… why now?"

"Mitch… I'm so terrified of what we may find and could possibly destroy us."

"I didn't want to tell you, but I talked with Burns this morning. I had him keep an eye on the light in the upstairs room…"

I watched his face and slowly said, "Go on…"

"The light was on last night, but I don't think we have anything to fear. The house seems content. We need to discover the mystery. I'll never let you go… ever, I promise no matter what… but we need to do this. Can you work with me, sweetheart?" He implored.

I shook my head okay. A verbal answer was not forthcoming. The light was still seen at night. This mystery had something not only to do with me, but with someone or something else… it had to be part of what Mitch's grandmother said. Now I knew this would be much harder for me. I had to come to grips with however it turned out. It was something we needed to know.

The panic began to rise inside of me when Mitch pushed on the secret panel in the right place and then pulled it open. The flashlights were ready and so was a battery operated lantern. We climbed the stone steps and hung the lantern on a nail.

Not a normal nail of today, but one which had been made in a blacksmith shop and hammered to create a head.

The lantern shone brightly over the room. There were rows

of books or ledgers on wooden shelves. The walls were made of stone. The room was secure and safe from water, wind, and sight.

There seemed to be strategically placed small openings, which allowed air to flow into the room. They were at the top of the ten by ten foot area with what appeared to be about seven foot in height. The room fit discretely between the ballroom and the library.

Mitch and I closely examined the room. This had to be where slaves had hidden in wait for Harriet Tubman to escort them to Philadelphia, as a conductor for the Under Ground Railroad. These were definitely beds, which hung from forged, metal chains and hooks in the ceiling. There were four such beds in the room. Without the books stored in the room, its size would have been adequate for a short stay.

The house was built in 1830 before the town was given the name Claiborne. Harriet moved her family from Caroline County in 1857. I was sure there had to be a ledger or diary about the people who'd passed through this house. She'd helped to set slaves free from 1850-1857, with travel by boats and railway. Back then, this room as a stopover, made thoughts of its usage by the Underground Railway an actual likelihood.

Mitch raised the larger flashlight high to see the room's contents better. My eyes focused on the far wall. Against the fortification in the back of the room was something wrapped in paper and string of some sort. Like a raffia.

"Mitch..."

"What, Kristen?" I could hear the anticipation in his tone.

"There's..." I couldn't seem to get the words to form. I

took a deep breath before I said, "Against the back wall, it's wrapped... like a bundle."

Mitch walked towards the bulky, draped package. He reached for it and brushed the layers of dust from the wrapping with his hand, handed me the flashlight and walked out of the room carefully, but with a struggle... since the size and shape were cumbersome for his freshly healed shoulder. I followed him into the library.

I trembled not sure what would be uncovered. He began gently and cautiously to remove the raffia from the package. His hands moved steadily to peel the paper, only to discover the parcel was also covered in what appeared to be a quilt. When the counterpane was removed it appeared to be a frame. I stood in front of him, but behind the picture. His facial expression told of dismay and shock.

"Mitch... what is it?"

He looked at me with an awareness I may become distressed, "I think we've found the portrait my grandmother spoke of... it's the portrait of Caroline." He said.

"How... do you know it's Caroline?" I asked with confusion.

He turned it slowly towards me and said, "Because... it looks exactly like you. It could be you. The hair your coloring and those eyes... they belong to you."

My hand raised slowly to my mouth in astonishment. I gazed upon the portrait, which most definitely could have been me. "Mitch... I... she..."

"She's beautiful indeed... like you. No wonder my grandfather, stared at this portrait most of the day. Somewhere among these ledgers has to be a diary and information about her. Who she was, where she came from, maybe you were related...?"

I felt faint. I wasn't sure if this was a great discovery or not.

Could this have been me? "Mitch... can we... take a break from this until tomorrow?"

He set the framed portrait aside and gathered me in his arms. "It will be okay, sweetheart. I'm as shocked as you. I thought my grandmother exaggerated about how much the two of you looked alike, and maybe there was a slight resemblance, or she blew this entire likeness out of proportion, but this is uncanny. We'll look through the books tomorrow."

I was concerned when I asked with skepticism, "Mitch, what will you do with this portrait?"

"I'm not sure... my thoughts are it would make my grandfather happy if it was hung in this house, but until I find out why the light remains on in the upstairs room... I don't know what to do."

Chapter 41

W e decided to endure the remainder of the day, upstairs in the pub. Mitch taught me how to shoot pool, we listened to the jukebox, and drank beer.

The beer was cold and after today's discoveries, I can say... I definitely had more than a few. With a kitchen in the pub area we had sandwiches for lunch. Tavern ham and Swiss cheese.

I wasn't normally a beer drinker, but they helped ease the tension we both felt. The portrait was discussed and it was decided... for now... to put it in the upstairs of the left wing sitting room, where the light has been seen.

He said it looked so much like me, we should hang it in the ball room or the dining room above the sideboard.

"Kristen, I want to tell you about the portrait of my father and of myself, which is now being painted and will soon occupy the wall with the other heads of family. All five generations of, Savage men."

"Mitch, this sounds wonderful. I know your father's initials are KSS. I know the K was for Kent, but the middle initial?"

"His middle name was Samuel, my grandmother's first name is Samantha, and of course the last name is Savage. My Grandfather was Mitchell Thomas Savage. His father... my great grandfather was Kent Mitchell. I was named after him. This is the linage so far."

He smiled and I knew what he referred to.

"Mitch, there was only one girl in the family... Mary. And all I can say is I hope we have at least one boy, but it could be a cluster of girls," I said. "The Savage men have ruled far too long."

I giggled at the expression of his first reaction, but then his smile said it wouldn't make a difference.

"Good then you are not opposed to children?" He questioned.

"No, I love kids. I guess we never discussed a family?" I replied. "It's not like we've had an abundance of time to become acquainted."

Now he snickered and reached his hands for me to come closer as he said, "No we didn't and I'm glad you want children. We have plenty of room for girls and boys."

I set my pool stick across the pool table and went into his opened arms. I softly whispered, "Maybe we should practice."

He kissed me fully on my mouth, looked at me with hunger in his eyes, and said softly, "It's the best idea I've heard all day." Was his enthusiastic response.

We rode the elevator downstairs. Mitch had my hand. We practically ran through the large room filled with windows, but void of furnishings, through the library to the main hall, and then up the stairs to our master suite.

"Mitch, I think we need an access from the pub to here." Was said in breathless anticipation.

His smile and blue eyes always seemed to unravel, "Sweetheart, it was done this way for security reasons. And, I'm here to make you feel secure." He declared.

No more was said... until we showered and dressed for dinner.

I may have had too much to drink, because I fell asleep in Mitch's arms after making love.

He didn't mind… he needed a nap too. The last few weeks had been very intense for him, concussion, stitches, gunshot wound, the move of all his possessions, and on top of all of this, business complications. I'm not going to mention the other things which had been on going and are… to this moment. But the nap was best for both of us.

Paul and his sous chef, Jason, prepared our meal.

At dinner we discussed our game plan for tomorrow on how to approach the secret room. We made the decision to go in, do what was necessary and not give up until we knew the mystery behind Windward Manor. After today's discovery I was apprehensive, but knew we needed to take care of this… to continue on with our lives.

Dinner was wonderful as expected. Paul was an exceptional chef. Mitch and I went to the study to relax for the evening, I refused a brandy tonight. I needed to check on my delivery for the shop. Our laptops were turned on. We'd promised each other we would take a few days to become adjusted to our new surroundings and one another. Here we were on our second night together focused on a portion of our jobs.

Both of our careers were a commitment and needed our attention. His was major. There were several hundred people he employed. After Christmas, I'd be finished in my shop until May.

"Mitch…?"

He looked up from his computer.

"What, sweetheart?"

"After we solve the mystery, can we start to plan our wedding?"

"Of course. I have a number of different thoughts, I'm sure you do too. There are a multitude of choices. We will travel once you close the shop and can be married anywhere and hold the reception here after our honeymoon."

I was excited to hear him divulge this information, I sat my laptop down, jumped off of the couch and said, "You mean we don't have to wait until May to get married?"

His laughter resonated through the house, "No we can be married anywhere we want and wait until May for the reception. That's my suggestion if you agree?"

He moved his computer... I climbed onto his lap. "Agree! I love the idea. I hate to wait. But wanted to hold the reception on the lawn. May seemed to be the perfect time. But I'd marry you at a Justice of the Peace!" I responded.

"Kristen, I'd marry you anywhere, anytime, you should know this by now... don't you?"

Those blue eyes embellished with long lashes, enthralled me. I had to move my body closer to his. Arms wrapped tightly around me. His kisses not only touched my heart, they touched my soul. He was truly all I'd ever need in my life, with only one exception.

Being able to marry when we wanted was a big deal for me. I'd wait for May, only because of my parents. I knew they wouldn't venture here in the winter and Mitch was sensible enough to know his grandmother would not attend—unless she got her wits about her.

By May we wouldn't care who showed up for the reception.

Tomorrow was another day.

Mitch waited for his computer to shut down when he looked at me and said, "Kristen, do you have any idea of all of the places we'll travel by the first of the year? All of these places are ports and offices to make sure KSS runs smoothly. We could be married in any one of the places you'd choose."

The list of cities was numerous.

"Where's our first stop," I asked. "I'd love to be married on a beach somewhere warm, you and me."

Mitch agreed and said he'd plan accordingly.

Chapter 42

It was a rainy day, the clouds filled the sky and the sunless heavens brought with it a peculiar sense of tension. I wish it could have been bright and sunny for the day's investigation into the ledgers and books we were determined to look through.

Mitch pushed and pulled on the undisclosed panel, to reveal the hidden room. We had two battery operated lanterns to see and read more clearly. They'd be hung on the hand fashioned nails, once in place I handed him two canvas director style folding chairs. We'd need a bit of comfort while we searched for information about Mitch's grandfather and Caroline.

After the two chairs were in place, I went up the three steps to take a seat, in the now, well lit room. I sat and Mitch began to see if the ledgers were organized by years, or randomly stored. We discovered… randomly stored… which would take us more time to research.

Mitch stacked a pile at my feet. I picked up the first ledger. It was of interest… it showed, cost, profit and loss. This ledger dated on the inside from May 1850 through September 1850. If they were all dated in such a fashion, maybe it wouldn't be quite as time consuming. We planned to stack them by dates after in-depth examination.

There was information on the crop growth and sales. Also

an expense ledger on the building of the main house, journals on payments to hired help, and food expense.

This all fascinated me... I loved history.

We took a break around noon for lunch since we'd started early this morning. It continued to rain and remained gloomy outside. After lunch Mitch and I went back to work. We didn't make a dent in all there was to leaf through. Maybe... we'd find a ledger or diary among the stack of books dated more recently... like in Kent Mitchell's era.

"Kristen, you can always come back and do a more thorough investigation on the history of Windward Manor. But for now check the date in the front of the book and move on to the next, until we come across what we're in search of."

We were to go to Jeanette's and Ethan's for dinner with Ava and Alex. The meal was set for 7:00 p.m. We needed to stop our search by 5:30 and return again tomorrow... unless we found something of importance.

I began to skim through the archives in case there was a hidden message on another form or loose sheet of paper, sandwiched between pages.

The ledgers we'd gone through were now in some semblance of order, for future reference.

Excitement coursed through my body when I came across what looked to be the journal, which held information on slaves Harriet Tubman helped send north.

It seems Harriet made eleven trips back to Maryland and on to Canada. The last entry was 1857, when she helped her niece Margaret to escape. Later the same year she helped her father Ben and her mother. They were the last to be hidden in this room until their escape could be successfully made.

"Mitch, there is so much history here. I can't believe what I've read."

"I know this information is of exceptional interest. But I also wonder how incriminating it is?" His expression looked worried. "I'm not sure if it's for the historical society of Claiborne or if we should keep it to ourselves." He added.

"It's been so many years ago," I replied. "But I'm sure these books and ledgers are valuable and need to be protected. I'm not so sure the historical society would be the safest place for this information. Maybe we should keep it quiet for a while... until we make the discovery we need."

He looked at me earnestly and said, "I think you may be right. There's so much information here on the town, the first settlers, history no one is aware of, you could compile enough information for a book to sell in your shop."

"Mitch, what a wonderful idea. I'd love to."

He looked at his watch and said, "Well the decision has been made, I think it's time to quit for the day.... and have fun with friends. What do you say?"

I was in agreement. I rose from my seat and grabbed the lantern closest to me, I made my way to Mitch. He held the other lantern. I left the hidden room first and he followed. The panel was pushed back into place. The history and the room would remain a secret for yet... another day.

Chapter 43

M itch and I were about ready to leave for Ethan's, when Burns dropped by to let us know he'd been accepted into Chesapeake College for the spring semester. He and Katie were together. They seemed to be a couple. I was happy for them. Burns said he loved the cottage and Katie planned to move in with him after Thanksgiving.

"Mr. Savage, will you need me? I want to take Katie to New York over the holiday weekend."

He was invited here for dinner and asked if he could bring Katie. After dinner they planned to leave for New York.

"Burns, I should be fine." Mitch responded. "And of course Katie is welcome to join us. By the way, you can do me a favor. I'll have Grace gather files and a few folders and have them ready for you to bring back. This way she doesn't have to mail them. They're important… I expect you to handle them accordingly."

"Certainly, sir. I guess then I need to stay in New York until at least Monday morning."

"I think it may be a good idea. It will give you and Katie an extra evening in the Big Apple. Will you two go to a Broadway show?" Mitch asked.

"We hadn't thought ahead, boss."

"Good, I'll have tickets for 'Mama Mia' on hold for Saturday evening. How would you two like to see the show?"

They were both all smiles and I think happy Mitch would gift them tickets for a night out.

"Thank you, sir, it'll be great."

Mitch looked at Katie and said, "Would you like to see the show?"

"Yes, I'd love it. I've never been to New York and look forward to the sights along with the decorated stores for Christmas, this is so much more—thank you, Mitch."

They knew we were headed out, they hugged me goodbye. Katie gave Mitch a hug and Burns and Mitch shook hands. Come to think of it my week in New York proved to be an experience of another nature. I didn't see a thing of interest. But I was there with Mitch and at the time… was what mattered most. He promised me another trip and I'd hold him to it.

Our evening with friends was great. It turned cold since it rained through the afternoon. It was a long day and tomorrow would be another—extensive day.

The shop needed to be opened. I'd decided to keep it closed thru the week and was pleased to have heard the UPS man earlier today when the doorbell rang, otherwise the items I'd ordered would have been soaked.

Tomorrow, I recruited Mitch's help with the decorations for the shop. He was needed to help carry and open the boxes I'd ordered.

We wouldn't be able to get back to our mystery until Monday, but thoughts were we could use the break. I've never seen so many volumes which held 185 years of history.

Now it was time for bed... and sleep. Mitch had other ideas... he handed me a brandy snifter. We sat together on the sofa and talked about our day and evening.

The brandy did its job, I was relaxed—because up until this point I'd had a hundred and one thoughts roll through my mind... now the only ones were of Mitch...

His good arm across my shoulder, left arm greatly improved, or I wouldn't allow him to carry boxes tomorrow.

Brandy finished. The glass removed from my fingers. A gentle kiss on the lips... hand in hand we walked upstairs to our bedroom. It was late. But never too late for love.

My cheeks felt hot, was it from the drink... or him.

I'd experienced sex before, but nothing like Mitch Savage. He brought out a part of me I'd never known. He was different in so many ways. All good and I was in love with him.

∽✦∾

Morning came too early. Neither of us wanted to roll out of bed. The sun was bright even though the temperature had dropped. There hadn't been morning strolls and wouldn't be again today.

Must be the nightly activity. We were worn out... of course the stress of probing for the mystery possibly added to our fatigue.

Hopeful our showers along with cups of coffee would resuscitate us and take hold... before the shop opened at 10:00 a.m.

By 9:30 a.m. we were on our way. Boxes carried in and opened. Some of the items were for Christmas and would be stored until after Thanksgiving. Mitch put those cases in the back room.

I thought if we decorated the shop today maybe Katie and Brittany would work tomorrow. I'd call and ask them. Mitch and I could not only sleep in, but continue to go through the volumes in the hidden room.

The day in the shop went by quickly. I placed items in their proper spaces, displays were arranged, and we stayed rather busy. Mitch was good with the customers. I wasn't surprised, because between his looks and personality he could sell these women the world.

I made contact with Brittany and she reached Katie, both girls were available to work tomorrow. Brittany came to pick-up the spare key and met Mitch for the first time. She was impressed with the new items we would sell for the Thanksgiving holiday... and I think... Mitch.

Before Brittany left with the key. She and I'd gone over the new items. Katie would be informed tomorrow. I'd be by later to close if needed and thanked her for coming to my rescue on such short notice.

"I need to give you girls more weekends to work." This was Mitch's suggestion. "Would you and Katie be interested?" I inquired.

Brittany replied, "Yes, but now Katie will be away the weekend after Thanksgiving."

"I'll see what I can work out, "I said. "I'm sure you two would like to earn extra money for the holidays."

Brittany smiled, "I would. Plus we're on semester break."

"I assume your first semester of college was what you expected and did you like it?" I asked

Her reply was, "I loved it.

After our discussion she left for home... it was time for Mitch and me to call it a day.

I didn't have to prepare a meal tonight. Mitch thought ahead and had Paul fix dinner. It may be a good idea while the shop remained opened to have him cook our meals... even if there wasn't company on the weekends

I loved for Mitch to be in the shop with me... but couldn't wait to get home. There would be a fine dinner when we arrived and tomorrow would be another day of exploration.

Chapter 44

S ince I wouldn't work in the shop today, we needed to get back to work in the secret room. Thursday was Thanksgiving... we didn't have much time to go through all the ledgers and journals.

Our morning was off to a great start and were able to sleep in, have a wonderful breakfast, and take a morning stroll. It was what I'd call a chilly day, but the sun was shining and its rays were warming... we walked hand in hand.

I loved being out in the sun and walk with Mitch. I'd had months before doing the same thing each day not aware of what was behind those boarded up windows, or who the owner was.

After our stroll, we'd set to work to look for more helpful information on Mitch's grandfather and Caroline. I checked on the girls at the shop and all was well.

Mitch and I returned to the house, removed our coats, the panel was opened and it was time to labor over more journals.

We hung the lanterns on the nails, which provided support. The lanterns gave off quite a bit of light. I took a seat in my chair and began my search.

I didn't find anything significant and neither did he. Soon

I was needed to close up the shop since I'd told Brittany I'd return.

The shop was closed and the girls said they'd had a good day. I dropped the deposit off at the banks night deposit and headed home. When I arrived home, Mitch was waiting. His usual striking smile when he greeted me… did not appear on his face.

"Mitch? What's wrong… did you find what we were looking for in one of the books?" I noticed the panel had been closed. There was a problem.

"Kristen, I need to be in New York. I'd like for you to accompany me. I don't want you here alone and Burns will be with me."

I didn't have to think about it and asked how long I had to pack. "Mitch… how much time, before we leave?"

"Can you be ready in an hour? Burns will take us to the airport. My plane should be ready for takeoff by the time we arrive. He will fly with us, so he can drive while we're in New York."

I ran upstairs, took a quick shower, threw personal items in a carry-on and grabbed the garment bag, which hung in the closet, packed with the outfits I took to New York the last visit.

Mitch paced. I walked to him, we stood toe to toe. My arms were around his neck. His went quickly around my waist and gathered me closer to him.

I softly said, "Mitch, what happened? You not only look upset, but I know you are."

"Kristen… it's my grandmother. She's had a heart attack." He spoke with distress.

I held onto him tightly, "Mitch, I'm sorry and want to be with you... but promise to stay out of her sight. I wouldn't want my being there to trouble her. Not now or ever."

He kissed the end of my nose and asked if I was ready, "Yes, I'm ready."

Mitch handled my garment bag and carry-on and by the time we reached the bottom step, Burns was in the driveway waiting for us.

I wondered if we'd be back in time for our Thanksgiving dinner and guests.

Brittany had the extra key to the shop, and if I wasn't back she'd need to not only open it, but arrange it's Christmas décor, and display such items.

We climbed into the backseat of the Mercedes and Burns didn't say a word, he was in work mode. He parked the car and we boarded the jet in record time. I sensed Mitch's concern for his grandmother. She was all he had left of his family and I needed to be with him.

Seated in the plush leather seats of his jet, he caught my hand and glanced at me.

"Mitch, she'll be fine. To know you'll be there will make her feel better."

"I don't know, Kristen. She's been disturbed over my move to Windward Manor and my grandfather."

"And me, Mitch. She was right. I do look like Caroline, but I'm not her." I responded.

"I know you're not. But we have yet to solve the mystery of who she was?" He said with torment.

This was not an ordinary plane and there wasn't a flight attendant. Burns told us take off would be in a few minutes, to make sure our seats were in an upright position and ready ourselves for departure. He took a seat and before I knew it we were moving down the runway. The last visit to New York was on a commercial flight and worried because my second sense said I hadn't been fully aware… how badly Mitch was wounded. Now he was distressed with thoughts of losing his grandmother.

The flight wasn't long. Before I realized it… we'd touched down. A limo was available for our ride to the hospital. Once we arrived at the hospital Burn's opened Mitch's door. He was out of the vehicle, but leaned in to speak to me and told Burns to take me to his place. I was under the assumption I'd also enter the hospital with him.

"Mitch, I want to be here for you."

"I'm okay. I want you to take a nap… rest. I'll be back in a few hours and we'll go to dinner. I'll call you when I leave the hospital. I love you, Kristen and I'm not going to let my grandmother stand in the way of our life. Relax. I'm in control of my emotions and know Gran has received the best care." He leaned towards me for a kiss. A grin spread over his face…"Love you."… and Burns closed the door.

Chapter 45

I wasn't surprised Mitch's choice of living in New York wouldn't be any less than elegant. Burns pulled up in front of The Carlton House with its limestone and brick exterior. He'd given me the key, the apartment number, and graciously helped me from the car. Our luggage was retrieved by the doorman. Burns instructed the doorman, to show me to Mr. Savage's apartment. This was an owned residence and had to be elaborate.

The doorman unlocked the door and opened it wide. I entered the gracious foyer. He followed behind with our luggage.

The place was sophisticated. My eyes scanned the white oak crafted floors and custom kitchen. I handed the doorman a tip, closed the door and locked it, walked through the large apartment to look outside. There was a lovely space for outdoor formal meals. The décor was on the same level, but a different style than the manor.

This was big city life.

I browsed through until I found the master suite. The white flooring was throughout the three bedrooms, with the exception of the bathrooms. They presented a black and white marble floor. The cabinetry lent itself to the chosen style of the floor. The view was magnificent from the 9th floor.

My cell phone rang, "Mitch?"

"Hi sweetheart, are you settled in?"

"Yes. This place is spectacular, I've …"

"It's spectacular because you're there… otherwise it has been a place to live. My grandmother's fine. All the tests came back normal, false alarm. I think she wanted to see me. I'm afraid she's taken a few years off my life—this being said, I'm on my way and will be to you shortly."

"Mitch…?"

"Yes, Kristen?" He answered softly.

"I don't want to take you away from your grandmother. How can we appease this situation?" I asked with distress.

"We'll talk about it over dinner. You should rest. I'll be with you soon." He said with emotion.

I tapped end on my phone. Rest? I couldn't rest, the excitement of the city engulfed me. I craved to see it all. The glass door to the open-air dinner space made it easy to view the well-lit skyline.

I heard Mitch come through the door and came out of the master suite to greet him.

With concern he asked, "Did I wake you?"

"No. I organized our closet and clothes. I was too excited to sleep and love this place, but even more now… you're here with me." I walked over and took Mitch's hand and asked, "You coming with me?"

I saw Mitch's gaze became dark and voracious. I gave a

surprised gasp when he scooped me up and headed to the master suite.

"It's not about words." Was the last thing I remember him saying.

We had reservations at Eleven Madison Park, a splendid restaurant with a unique experience. This was the first really big date we'd been on. I didn't think crabs and pizza were real dates, although the chef we had at home—I'd consider a dinner date.

This evening gave me the opportunity to wear a dress from my garment bag, which I didn't have the opportunity on my last visit. Mitch loved my funky, mid-thigh, black and white fringe tank dress, my deco earrings and the black leather ankle, peep-toe boots with their four inch heel. I wouldn't have worn this ensemble... unless somewhere trendy and New York was the place. My short faux fur jacket was needed... the temperatures had plummeted.

Mitch helped me remove my jacket and checked it. Once we were seated I let him choose what we'd eat. He said he'd been here before. A streak of jealousy washed through me and wondered who the lucky girl had been, but we had more important issues to discuss. One huge subject was his grandmother. Did I really want a conversation about her right now? I'd wait until Mitch brought it up first.

We had desert. He began to speak about his grandmother... before this point in the evening it had been pleasant and about us. When he began I was prepared to listen.

"Kristen, this so called heart attack of my Gran's was brought on by her stubbornness. Of course I've dated before, but no one on a serious level and no one closely related to Windward Manor. Your resemblance to Caroline, my move, all these things have upset her. I was firm and said there would be no compromise. My move was one of permanence and my love for you wouldn't change. Gran listened and said she knew I was strong willed and had my own sense of right and wrong. If I felt you were the woman I loved, she wouldn't come between us, but her judgment on you would remain the same." He reached for my hand across the table. "Sweetheart, we were given her blessing. It was also relayed to me not to count on her to visit Windward Manor, nor would we see her at our wedding. I assured her this was fine, but I'd promised to visit once in a while and telephone her."

"Mitch, do you seriously believe, with her age, you'll be comfortable with this decision?" I asked.

"Kristen, we lived in the same city... with work and travel I didn't see her often and we only spoke once a month. She knows I'm busy, has her friends, and a brother here. She'll do fine. I never want her to interrupt what we have. You come first. If you need me, I won't visit with her—but when we're here... and I'm able... I will."

"Mitch, I wouldn't hold you back. She has played a huge part in your life and you may need to be with her." I responded with sincerity.

"True, but I also understand she's the one who chased my mother out of our lives. She was possessive then and now. I can't allow it." He became very serious. "I won't be without you… in my life."

No more was said about his grandmother. The rest of the evening was wonderful. We'd leave on Wednesday, just in time for our first Thanksgiving dinner in Windward Manor.

Chapter 46

Mitch said he'd show me New York, and after Christmas we'd travel to San Francisco. He expected me to show him my old town. A deal was made and I'd have to say we had a fabulous and remarkable time until his jet took off from New York and returned us to Maryland.

Wednesday's arrival in Maryland was early enough to assist in the Thanksgiving Day preparations. Next year we'd stay in New York for the Thanksgiving Day parade.

I'm not quite sure what preparations Mitch referred to, because Paul had it under control and the only thing left for us to do—was take a long nap.

"Mitch, did I tell you what a wonderful time I'd had. We didn't stop once we got started. Between the Broadway Shows, the sights, food in so many different, and diverse restaurants… I'm sure I've gained a few pounds."

"We did a lot of walking, Kristen." He responded.

"Yes, you're right, but the meals we ate were a definite no-no for the waistline."

He couldn't help but laugh at me. Then he reminded me,

"You know the decision we make on our way home. The one to be married in Belize in early February."

I shook my head yes, and went into his arms.

The smile on his face was unbelievable. He gathered me close and said, "Well there's more. The end of December for New Year's Eve we'll be in San Francisco. You'll have the chance to show me your turf, Kristen. And from there we'll visit a few ports for KSS and end up in Belize by February."

"It all sounds incredible, Mitch."

"We'll be on the move from San Francisco, Mexico, Costa Rico, and Guatemala. I think you need to shop for a warm weather wardrobe. So many places will be warmer than here." He stated with excitement.

Right now my mind was overwhelmed with thoughts of where we'd travel to… and I said, "Yes, now I need a nap."

"Sweetheart, I want nothing more than to climb into bed right this minute, feel your heart beat next to mine and know we're home. I don't need any more… at least not right now."

He looked like a little boy with dreamy eyes and huge dreams.

We slept until dinner. When we woke, the smell of Thanksgiving Day pies filled the air. Casually dressed we were to eat at the harvest table in the kitchen.

For our meal Mitch had requested Paul to grill us each a portion of fish, baked sweet potato, along with a healthy salad. We needed to get back to an improved diet.

While in New York, Mitch said he had a surprise for me. Since we weren't home I was told we'd had furniture delivered for the room with the most absolute fantastic view of the grounds, the bay, and the bridge from the wall of windows. Our guests wouldn't have to be crammed into the study tomorrow. He'd had a designer friend from New York choose comfortable and relaxed furnishings for the large room not only suitable to the area, but to the balance of the house.

"Mitch, before dinner, how about you show me the furniture?" I said with excitement.

He took my hand and down the stairs we went. He drew me through the wide hallway, into our TV room and library, and through the open doorway of the adjacent wing.

"So... what do you think?" He appeared so proud of himself.

"It's beautiful," I replied. "Between the dining room for the meal, the windowed room and the pub, our guests should have an excellent time."

"I'm glad you like it. I chose it before there was an *us*." It was said as an apology.

"I think it's perfect." I responded.

Our night before Thanksgiving dinner was great, just what Mitch ordered. When we finished, we relaxed in the study. We sat close together and talked about Friday and how we'd make every attempt to finish the quest for any and all informative documents which would lead us to unravel the mystery of Windward Manor.

I was hopeful we'd find data to make his grandmother happy and want to return for a visit. There wasn't much on TV, we went to the pub room to shoot pool, and listen to the jukebox.

The new furniture looked fantastic, but the room was too big for us to use on a daily basis. It would be our great room for parties and friends.

Mitch and I finally had the chance to dance together in New York. After a few games of pool, he played a song we both loved on the jukebox and we slow danced. It had been a long three and a half days.

The jukebox was turned off, pool sticks hung up, and we went to check the dining room to make sure it was set for our guests. Then we slowly, with arms around one another, went upstairs for the night.

I came out of the bathroom... Mitch stretched on the bed, blankets to his waist... waited for me. His chest exposed all sinewy muscle, flat stomach, wide shoulders, and narrow hips. His beautiful blue eyes, watched my every move. I peeled off my robe, let it pool at my feet... and approached him

"Mitch, I think you have what I need to help me fall asleep."

"I know I do, sweetheart," Was his response.

His hand stretched out to me... pulled me across the bed to him. There was a magnetic attraction since I'd first met him... just to look at him, and those blue eyes... once cold as ice, but at any given moment burned with a heat of passion, made me want him even more... my mind filled with thoughts of our first night together. He was the kind of man who could give love, make a woman feel desired... and protected. I'd always need and want him. I prayed his grandmother wouldn't tear us apart.

When Mitch woke me with a kiss, we were entwined from last night. Softly he said, "Sweetheart, you may want to begin to ready yourself for our first dinner party."

"Oh, Mitch—I had the nicest dream about you. I'm not ready to wake up." I pleaded.

His kisses began to intensify. I knew there was no way to get out of bed now, we had hours before we'd need to entertain our guests.

Chapter 47

O ur company arrived. The house was filled with wonderful aromas, laughter, and conversations. Until we'd gather in the dining room for dinner, the new room and the pub were being put to use.

It seemed the younger crowd favorited the pub and the older guests enjoyed the view along with the sun's radiant warmth which shined through the windows... on this cold November day.

The room alluded warmth with the soft-buttery colored leather furniture. It fit perfectly to permit the friendliness of the group to view one another as they conversed. The oriental patterned rug with its array of pale colors displayed in the center and the floor allowed the furniture which surrounded it... to mark the perfect venue for the room.

We had time for happy hour and then the dinner bell rang to signify the meal was being served. Taken back upon entry to the dining room when my eye caught the portrait above the sideboard.

The portrait of Caroline commanded the attention it was given. It owned the place in which it hung.

With question I observed Mitch, he grabbed my hand and softly said, "She's been hidden away far too long. Her presence in this room is perfect... no one will know it's not you. We won't have to explain a thing."

Comments were made not only about the portrait, but about the dramatic table setting, and meal, which had been placed on the banquet size table. I had to agree the portrait complemented the room and its furnishings.

A prayer was said by Mitch and thoughts of a meal in this room many years ago crossed my mind. Looking at the picture I wondered if I may have been here. To think this meal had been recreated with new friends and hopefully one day with a family of our own.

Throughout the meal I'd gaze upon Caroline's expression and knew we'd have to soon discover her secret. I prayed the outcome of this mystery would bring Mitch, his grandmother, and me... closer together.

Friday was here. It was time to pursue our search. Yesterday was such a wonderful time, I hated for it to end. Of course it had a happy ending, but now it was time to get to work.

I rubbed my eyes. I didn't think I was fully awake and ready to take on this endeavor. Mitch was about to open the panel in the wall when the doorbell chimed. I looked at him and a smile crossed his face. What did he have going on in his mind?

We walked to the front door. Mitch opened it. There were two packages which needed to be signed for. They were in cardboard cartons and quite large.

He signed for the packages and I could sense his excitement. "Mitch, what did you buy?"

He began to open the first of the boxes, "Kristen, these are the two portraits to finish the staircase for now. I'll unwrap and hang them before we proceed with our search."

"Oh! Wow... I can't wait to see them. Whoever you hired to paint... had to capture the blueness of your eyes?"

"We shall see. The artist came highly recommended." He stated

The cartons were opened. Mitch's father resembled his ancestors. Mitch unwrapped his portrait. I was right he was the most handsome of all the men and his eyes were the most perfect shade of blue.

"It's an exact likeness of you, the artist did a fabulous job. These will look wonderful on the wall." I responded with excitement.

Mitch grabbed a hammer and the correct hangers for the portraits. He must have been aware they'd been shipped... he was prepared. The paintings finished off the staircase and the five generations of the Savage heads of family... were exceedingly—handsome men.

It was time for lunch. A turkey sandwich, mayonnaise, lettuce with salt and pepper was the choice and a thin slice of pumpkin pie, topped with real whipped cream for dessert. We looked at one another and tried to decide if we'd need a nap... but couldn't put off the inevitable any longer.

The panel was opened and the lanterns were hung.

I asked, "By chance was there a date on the back of, Caroline's portrait?'

"No." He replied. "Nothing at all to begin to even give us a clue. The only way we know anything about her is because my grandmother said you looked like her and called you Caroline."

We were in our chairs and began our search. After a few hours of not finding anything other than profit, cost and loss ledgers, Mitch left to bring us each a drink. He returned quietly. I was absorbed in my investigation of a paper I'd found stuck between the pages of a ledger.

I heard before I saw him, "God, you're beautiful."

I glanced up with tears in my eyes. I'd never known a love like his, and the tears were not only from what he'd said, but from what I'd just read.

"Mitch, no one has ever said anything like this to me, only you. It means so much to hear it from you because… you know my last relationship left me feeling insecure and doubtful of my worth as a woman. Not only are these tears from what you've said, but I've found something and it elicited tears of sorrow, for what must have been an unspeakable torment to your great grandfather."

Mitch knelt and leaned closer, set my drink on the stone floor beside me, and pulled me to him. I tried to suppress my sobs.

"Can you tell me. Or do you want me to read it?" He asked.

I held up the paper, "I found this stuck between the pages of the ledger. It's the invoice or bill from the artist who painted Caroline's portrait. The note jotted on it as best I can tell says, *My beloved wife, who died giving life.* It's dated around your grandfather's birth."

He stood and paced in the small area, "We need to find a diary. This was not my grandfather's love, but his fathers." He raised his eyes to me in question and love. "Do you think she may have died giving birth to my grandfather? Caroline could be grandfather's mother?" He stopped his stride and came towards me again, his hands held onto the armrests of my wooden chair. "Kristen, this is why he loved this portrait so much. I know he was the firstborn of five sons and given this house. Is it possible his stepmother never truly accepted him?"

"Mitch, it all sounds probable." I covered his hands with mine gently and searched his eyes. "We have to continue our search. Your grandfather was Mitchell Thomas and his father was Kent Mitchell, the younger son of the first Savage. Nowhere in the history of Windward Manor was Caroline ever mentioned. All the history books say his wife was Adeline."

"Kristen, do you think you can continue. I know you're upset, but I'd like to see if there is anything else we can find, related dates of marriage to Caroline or Adeline."

"If we don't find it here maybe there are records in the old church in town, Mitch?" I replied.

Chapter 48

We felt we were on the right path, but needed to continue to look through each leather bound book. I was exhausted for the day, Mitch closed up the wall panel to the hidden room and we were to have leftovers for dinner. Both of us mentally drained.

A letter, a diary, anything to tell us when his grandfather may have been told about his birthmother needed to be found and when he was aware there was a portrait of her.

My mind was boggled because we still had no idea why the light was lit in the upstairs room, why the house seemed unhappy at times, and welcoming at others.

Mitch and I cleaned up dinner together. It was late and I was needed to open the shop tomorrow and place Christmas displays in the appropriate locations. Brittany would help me since Katie was in New York with Burns. Mitch was to have Burns check on his grandmother while he was there.

There would be no TV tonight merely a shower and bed for us. I wasn't sure if Mitch would come with me to the shop tomorrow. Thoughts were he may have work to do on his laptop since we'd brought back a pile of files from New York. Burns could cross it off his to do list… and enjoy his visit.

It dawned on me on our way upstairs, when I peered into the dining room. Caroline was Mitch's great grandmother and she did belong in this house.

"Mitch, I'm glad you brought Caroline's picture down from upstairs, she rightfully deserves to be seen."

"You know through all of our searches it hadn't registered in my mind she was my great grandmother. Thank you for the reminder. But I still can't believe how the two of you look identical. My great grandfather and I both had great taste in women… hope we're not related."

This distressed me, "Oh, Mitch… don't say such a thing. We have no idea of her background, where she was from or her last name. I don't want to be related to her in any way it would keep us apart. I look like her and you have the same name as your great grandfather. Could this be…"

"Kristen, I know things here are beyond weird but…"

He hesitated for a moment before he said… "Do you know your families heritage, where they're from. Can you find out about your family tree… now you have me worried?"

"You… I won't be able to sleep until we know the entire story. My father is Welsh and mother is German her maiden name was Adler. Dad's family settled in California. I'm not so sure when my mother's family settled there, but that's where they met. Most of the people who settled on the Chesapeake Bay were English." I believed.

"Well, this makes me feel better, sweetheart. Maybe we can sleep after all." His smile said he had something on his mind. "But if we can't…" He pulled me close and kissed me, I headed to the shower, he followed.

It was 8:30 a.m., past time to rise and shine. I wanted to head early to the shop to set up a few of the Christmas displays and put the Thanksgiving items on the sale rack. But first my eyes needed to adjust to the morning light, which filtered through the slightly opened curtains. By the time I'd shower, dress, have my coffee and eat, there wouldn't be much time to set up the shop.

I asked softly, "Mitch, did you turn off the alarm clock?"

Entwined in his arms the response was, "Guilty…we needed the extra sleep."

"And whose fault was it?" I asked kiddingly.

He answered tenderly, "Yours… being near you is the problem sweetheart, but I'm going to start my day by following you to the shop to help… and then I'll return here and catch up on my work. What do you say?"

"I say wonderful, because otherwise it would be a very long day without you."

His smile and those blue eyes set me to kiss his gorgeous lips, but then jump out of bed.

"Kristen, get back here!" He bellowed.

"No… we have to be up and on the move if we are to get anything done today. What did Paul decide to make for dinner tonight?" I hollered on my way to the bathroom.

"I don't know. He was told to surprise us. Let me know when you're out of the shower and I'll get in while you dry your hair." He said.

I yelled back, "Okay."

We reached the shop by 9:30 a.m. with a coffee and a muffin from the coffee shop across the street. Not the best breakfast, but I'd order a better lunch. Mitch brought in the Christmas boxes from the back room. We did at least move Thanksgiving items to an area for sale and now we had a place to display Christmas. When Brittany arrived, Mitch left me with a kiss. She and I began to set the exhibit.

By lunchtime, we'd had quite a bit of traffic through the shop and the empty objects were restocked. It had been a profitable morning. Brittany was to go to lunch first and then it was my turn. Even though the day was busy, we were organized. If Katie would be here tomorrow… I wouldn't need to work and wanted so badly to look for more evidence in the mystery room.

We closed at 4:00 p.m. The deposit was dropped off at the banks night slot and I headed home. Mitch was missed terribly. I drove up to the house and let myself in and called for him. There was no answer. He was found in the hidden room. I spoke to him from the open door.

"Mitch, I couldn't find you. What made you decide to do this today?"

"I needed to make sure we weren't related and found the ledger dated before you found the note and receipt. I've found the original order for the portrait. My great grandmother's full name was Caroline L. Madison Savage. She and great grandfather seemed to have been married at least a year before her death by the dates written in the ledger. I don't think there is any type of relation between the two of you, except for your looks."

"Thank God. I guess it's the most wonderful news out of this entire mystery." I exclaimed.

He came out of the room, picked me up, and kissed me. "It's the best news, baby. We're on the right track. Anyway we now know who Caroline was. How was the shop today? Were you busy?"

"Yes, it was a little crazy. I continued to replace the sold merchandise. It was a good day, but I missed you and asked Mrs. Chester if she'd be interested in working with Brittany tomorrow… she said yes… so we have all day tomorrow to be together. What do you think?" I countered.

"I love it already." He said and held me tightly. "By the way Paul was here. He's prepared a salad and a turkey casserole for dinner. He asked if we'd mind placing it in the oven for an hour before we were ready to eat." Mitch set me away from him to turn on the oven. "Soooo… I thought we could have a happy hour with a glass of wine or two, to relax us while the casserole bakes. " He said.

"I like the idea. But after this casserole I don't want to hear the word turkey again." I replied.

Mitch, pulled me back into his arms and hugged me. We both laughed.

"Paul said he didn't want to waste what was left of the second turkey, it was all white meat and you'd love it. I told him to take the remains home and he could make his family turkey noodle or whatever they made with the carcass of the bird. I'm with you, no more turkey for a while."

The casserole, which smelled wonderful— was to bake for an hour. The bottle of wine and two glasses went with us into the study, our feet were propped up… after Mitch closed the secret panel.

Chapter 49

S unday morning felt exceptionally delightful. The shop was taken care of, already showered, breakfast made, eaten, and now a cool morning walk with Mitch was in order. We each had our insulated coffee mugs filled and out the door we went.

A decision was made to sit on the pier and let our legs dangle. The water was calm and the tide was out. It was a way to relax before we started our search in the hidden room. There were quite a few books to leaf through, but thoughts were if we persevered the secrets and mysteries of the manor by days end may be known.

We didn't stay outdoors long because it was a penetrating, damp kind of cold. Winter was on its way. I was looking forward to migrate to the warmer climates with Mitch. We had our passports in order and needed to find the requirements to be married in Belize... to make sure it would be legal.

Mitch heard my teeth chatter and wrapped his arm around me, "What do you say, babe, how about we go inside, stand by the fire get all nice and toasty, and begin our work for the day?"

I looked at those blue eyes of his and heat passed through my body, "I'm ready when you are." I stated.

We walked from the pier. Down the wooden steps, onto the sand, up the slight knoll, to the stone stairs, up the few steps, and opened the black ornate gate, which led us onto the stone walkway to the house. My insulated coffee cup fit perfectly inside his… he held both cups and my hand.

Summer would be beautiful when the grass would be green, lush, the landscape complete, and the flowers which would come with the warmer weather. The gradual entry pool would be most accommodating and thoughts of our wedding reception would be fantastic… in this incredibly attractive site.

We entered the house. It's warmth was welcomed. I slid my jacket off. Mitch took the coffee cups to the dishwasher and slipped off his jacket. It was time for work. The panel was opened and our lanterns were lit. We hoped today would be the day to find exactly what we were in search of.

My fingers were crossed.

It seemed Mitch had gone through a good number of books yesterday by himself. I read more of what was in the ledgers than was necessary. Today I'd check dates, shake the books gently, and see if anything of importance falls out.

The shelves the books had been on were now partially empty, a few ledgers remained on the floor in neat piles. Others had been placed in order by dates, back on the shelves. Mitch and I split the piles and began our search.

It seemed like forever when we finally took a break and indulged in lunch.

"Mitch, do you think we'll ever get through the mounds of records. They were kept since the 1830's and I'm sure up until the day your grandfather passed away. Once they are in order, I'll look more closely and create a book on Windward Manor and the town of Claiborne."

My cell phone rang, it was Jeanette.

"Hi! Are you up for crabs tonight? Ethan had jumbo's delivered today."

I looked at Mitch and asked him, he said, "Yes. My shoulder is better and I can pick my own ... and I'm sick of turkey."

I was too. We laughed

"Invitation accepted, Jeanette. We've had it with turkey."

We'd work for a while and then close up the room... tomorrow would be another day.

Ava and Alex, were already at the Crab Shanty, along with Jeanette, and Ethan, when we arrived. Mitch and I each had a cold beer and warm crab dip with pita chips while at the bar and waited for the crabs to steam.

Ethan had Will steam the crabs tonight. He said he was not working. Tonight he's one of us.

He thanked me for asking his mom to work today. "She loves the shop and enjoys the work. The best part was to meet, greet, and chat with the tourists."

I knew she and Brittany had a great day when told the amount of the deposit. It was nice of Ethan's mother to take it to the bank for me... this way I wouldn't have to return to the shop. She was to watch Cory, tonight. It was the six of us. We'd become great friends.

During the laughter and conversation, Jeanette asked, "Why, are you not wearing the beautiful necklace you sported when the portrait was painted? I noticed it—and thought you could wear it with almost everything."

I touched my neck out of shock and had no idea what to say. Mitch overheard Jeanette's question and kiddingly said, "I love to kiss on her neck... it would be in the way."

Of course those who heard the question and answer thought it was funny and laughed.

Questions not only about the necklace, but the portrait itself had been raised. They couldn't comprehend how Mitch found an artist to turn the painting around so quickly and was the necklace an heirloom?

Mitch gave a quick response, "I had two other portraits also commissioned by the same artist to complete the lineage on the staircase."

Everyone was astonished at how beautiful my portrait turned out and couldn't wait to see the other two.

Thankfully we heard, "Everyone be seated, here come the crabs, they're hot, be careful."

Ethan made this announcement, then we took a seat at the round table. I was grateful the conversation about the portrait and necklace had passed.

Now the conversation was about how much longer Ethan would be able to receive crabs and other seafood. Later we remarked about the change in wedding plans, how we decided to be married in Belize and the reception would be held in late May when the temperature was warmer.

I saw the enthusiasm in their eyes.

Ethan was first to say, "You know come February, Jeanette and I could use a good vacation, we never had a honeymoon."

Alex said he and Ava would be ready for some warm weather also, did we mind if they joined us.

Mitch and I looked at one another and said, "Yes... yes, it would be wonderful to have you along."

I added, "Mitch has an itinerary, but not quite completed. We'll leave after the holidays, with stops to make in different ports along the way. Give us another week, by then he'll have it narrowed down to the date of arrival and how long we'll be able to stay in Belize."

Alex asked, "Any chance for two weeks? I could use a nice long vacation."

They all seemed to be in agreeance, two weeks. I looked at Mitch and his smile said why not.

I was excited, to be married among friends in Belize... of all places. It would be perfect.

Chapter 50

M onday morning, not a chance for a stroll. Clouds and rain, a miserable day outside. The fireplace was crackling. We were back to the hidden room to search through more of the ledgers.

Besides the careful turn of each page, I'd shake the book gingerly to see what may be hidden between. The pile of journals became smaller… the size reduced. I began to feel fervent… we were close to the secret. I couldn't stand to be seated any longer and had to get up… move around for a second.

"Mitch, we're so close… I can feel it. I'm happy this is coming to an end, but unhappy as to what the reason may be behind the fact your grandfather never brought your grandmother and his son back here to live."

Mitch grabbed my hand and pulled me onto his lap. I sat with my head on his shoulder… he kissed my cheek.

"Baby, I hope if we find the answer we can both live with it and give my grandmother peace. Do you want to take a break? It's not quite lunch time."

"No. I'll be okay. Thanks for the kisses they helped immensely."

I sat back in my chair and picked up a different bound book, shook it slightly and a few folded papers fell out. "Mitch…" I said softly with great hope. "I've found something. Do you want me to read it to you or do you want to read it?" I asked.

"You read it, Kristen. Let me look at the book." He said.

I handed him the book and began to read. The script in which it had been written was conducive to the time period and hard to decipher. I read it over twice before I told Mitch what it said.

"Mitch, this is a letter to your grandfather from his father, he tells him Caroline was his birthmother and the love he had for her. She dies when she gave birth to him. He was sorry your grandfather never had the chance to meet her. How Caroline would have loved him."

I stopped to look at Mitch's face before I continued to relay the letter in my own words. "He tells your grandfather of the portrait… where it's hidden… about the secret room… the journals, and the rooms past. This must have been given to your grandfather when his father was on his deathbed."

Mitch looked at me intently I wasn't sure what he found or was about to say.

"Kristen… this is my grandfather's diary."

The passion in his voice made my heart skip a beat.

"It appears my grandfather's memoir was started after he obtained ownership of this house. I need to read more. But what I've read so far … he knows now why the woman he referred to as his mother went to Virginia to join his brothers after his father's death. He mentions the fact he has no one except a portrait of his mother to gaze upon and tells how it gives him such pleasure."

Mitch had tears in his eyes, so did I, and was sure if we read further into the diary we'd learn more.

We put the rest of the ledgers in order, brought out the

battery operated lanterns and chairs from the secret room, closed the panel on the history of Windward Manor.

Now we'd read and hopefully understand its mystery.

Mitch and I went to the kitchen for lunch and when we finished we'd read from his grandfather's diary... in the warmth of the study... on this gloomy, but inspirational day.

We sat close together... he read page after page about how lonely his grandfather's life had been. How most of his life he felt he didn't belong and by the time he was forty he found a love, one he could not believe entered into his life. He'd watch her from the window in his bedroom. Since he was the eldest, his room was at the end of the hall in the left wing. He read and helped with the figures in the ledgers from this room when he was a young man.

Once his father passed and his family moved to Virginia, he felt comfort in the room from his youth and stayed there as he aged. How he'd seen a young woman and she caught his eye. He was much older than she, but was fascinated by her.

He'd asked her father if she could work in his home as his maid. The father was more than happy since they could use the money to feed her siblings. They were tenants in the overseer's cottage.

"Mitch, she lived in my house, your grandmother lived there, which could be why he has watched the cottage until now, but this doesn't fully explain it. Keep reading, I know the answer lies in his diary."

Mitch went on to read, 'Samantha worked hard and was shy, but I was impressed with her. The portrait of my mother hung in my sitting area for a while. Once Samantha and I became closer I placed my mother's portrait in the dining room to feel close to her and moved my belongings to the center sector of the house. I was in love with Samantha and she finally showed affection towards me. Even thought she would go home at night I couldn't wait for her return each morning.'

"Kristen, he talks about when he first kisses her and they engage in a sexual relationship. When she became pregnant and how he becomes worried about her dying during childbirth. What would he do without her, how he'd sit and stare at his mother's portrait for guidance."

I heard the catch in Mitch's voice... he continued, "He was a loner and there was no one to talk too. How they went to Virginia to marry and...here it is, Kristen. He writes *Samantha seemed unhappy and disappeared only to be found in New York. My attorney sent her money. I sit each night in my room in the left wing, and wait for her return.*

I was in tears. "He died of a broken heart and your grandmother thought all this time he didn't love her. He must be at peace now knowing I look like his mother and have come to live here. This is sad and unbelievable, Mitch, it hurts my heart so. Your grandmother needs to read this and understand how much he loved her. If she came back he'd be so pleased— the light may go off in his room. His spirit could finally find peace"

"I know... but where to begin for her to comprehend?"

"You need to go to New York, and force her read his diary or read it to her, tell her like you told me... she has to listen. Mitch, this would mean so much for us. We could live as a family and not have her hate me."

With a sense of hope he said to me, "Kristen, I want to leave my grandfather's rooms untouched upstairs, will you mind if they're not remodeled?"

I shook my head, "No. I don't mind at all. Do you have any idea what furniture was in his rooms? We could put a fresh coat of paint on the walls and put everything back the way it was." I said.

"Yes… I know what was in there and can bring it down from the attic for him."

I embraced Mitch and held him close, this was such a huge discovery and could see it meant the world to him and… to me.

Chapter 51

M itch arranged a trip to see his grandmother. Of course I was going to stay in his apartment until he could relay the entire story to his grandmother. At which point I hoped she'd accept me as Kristen and not see me as Caroline. Who truly knew if I was once Caroline. We looked so much alike. But… this was something else entirely.

We had a few days before we'd leave for New York. Mitch had paperwork to complete for KSS. We continued to make wedding plans which included our group of friends. I had to work this weekend and then we'd be on our way.

I realized on our way upstairs for the night, Mitch and I would hold separate conversations with the portraits along the wall. He caught me telling his grandfather, we'd bring Samantha back for a visit.

At this point Mitch grabbed me and said, "I've also told my grandfather and father… life in Windward Manor would be spectacular once again. I'm sorry my father didn't have the chance to live and grow up here, but my life here with you, will be full of love."

Of course Mitch was more than amorous since the mystery had been solved and if we weren't careful, I could end up pregnant before we were married. I didn't care... he gathered me in his arms, and carried me up the stairs... his ancestors looked on.

I'd readied myself for bed, he came to me from the bathroom picked me up and placed me on the bed, leaned over, and pressed a gentle kiss on my lips. I looked up at him and his blue eyes held me in his sights as heat passed through my soul.

Clothes peeled from his exceptional body... he climbed into our bed next to me... pulled my night gown slowly and deliberately over my head... drew me closer so our naked bodies touched.

There was much I needed to say to him, but he silenced me with his mouth, while his hands roamed my body... igniting a fire within my depth. I took a breath which had been captured inside and whispered, "I love you." And for the first time I felt I was truly home.

Home in the house I'd fantasized about for most of my life and now I knew the secret of Windward Manor... but never expected him to be a part of my dreams and fantasy in a million years.

Mitch was busy at his desk. I was curled into the corner of the leather sofa with the phone, ready to call my mother.

I'd gotten his attention and asked, "Do you think before we run off and get married you should meet my parents?"

"Babe, I think it might be a good idea." He responded.

"Can we fit a few days in Arizona on our way to San Francisco?" I asked.

He laughed, "No problem, what's a few more days tacked on to the beginning of our trip? I'll merely need to alert the pilot of the change in plans."

"Okay, I thought it might be the right thing to do. They need to know I'm engaged and when and where we'll be married."

It was past time to inform my mother of my plans and the mystery behind the manor. Being an only child I wasn't sure if my father would miss walking me down the aisle. Neither one of them seemed to be excited when I told them about Mitch. I expected they had their own agenda and to walk me down the aisle wasn't at the top of their list. My father had worked hard his entire life as a waterman. I understood they finally had time to relax.

They both deserved it.

I called and chatted with my mom. I began to tell her we'd solved the mystery of the manor, my engagement, and plans for our wedding.

"Mom, Mitch, and I'd like to visit you and Dad after Christmas, would it be okay? We'll be headed to San Francisco on business and on our way I'd like for you to meet him."

There was silence on the phone for a few minutes and then I heard her ask my father if he wanted to meet Mitch and when we'd be coming.

"Mom, we don't have to stop. I thought it would be nice if you met him. We'd stay in a hotel. It wouldn't be any work for you."

"That's not the problem. Your father has plans to take me

on a cruise after Christmas and I'm not sure of the dates. Of course we want to meet Mitch, but let me make sure the dates don't conflict or we'll see you at the reception."

"Oh…okay. Let me know."

I hung up the phone and looked at Mitch.

He looked at me.

"I have no idea what's up with them, it's almost like they want to do their own thing. I guess they figure I'm old enough to make my own decisions… and I am, but it's weird."

"Sweetheart, if I know a week before we leave, I can make arrangements. Don't worry about it, we'll be fine. You've been on your own for so long they probably don't know how to handle your need to be in their lives again." He consoled.

"Yes—you could be right. I never did come home for holidays or any events in years. I'm okay with whatever they decide because I have you. And especially nights like last night."

Mitch winked and gave a loud chuckle.

Chapter 52

W e were on our way to New York. Mitch's grandmother was told he would come to visit her, but not why. I'd keep my fingers crossed she accepted what he'd tell her and would receive me.

Life would be great if we could have a family Christmas at Windward Manor this year. I wasn't so sure my parents would leave the warmer climate to come home for the holiday, but they said they'd be away after... so perhaps Christmas in Claiborne wouldn't interfere in their plans.

Our friends would be invited for a gala Christmas Eve party and dinner the next day. The house would be filled with scents of the holiday, family and friends.

We'd talk about plans once he informed his grandmother of our discoveries.

We traveled by way of Mitch's jet, Burns and Katie were still in New York, because Mitch asked him to stay and Katie wasn't ready to come home without him.

Burns was to pick us up from the airport and take Mitch to his grandmother's and me to the apartment. But there was a change in plans. It was late, we were tired and he'd see his grandmother in the morning.

Mitch was asleep... a short nap before we reached New York. I began to think... seriously think, about how Samantha would take this revelation. She had to tell her son about his father and why he never had the chance to meet him. I wonder what she'd said, and now he was no longer with us to ever know... the truth.

When we returned home I'd have to tell my friends the truth about the portrait and why the light was lit in the upstairs room, Ethan may have been the only one to know. Now when I think about it... where was the necklace.

Mitch stretched his arms in the air. I knew the way he'd held them crossed in front of him, they'd be stiff when he woke.

He sounded alarmed when he said, "Kristen... you're awake? I thought for sure you'd rest until we reached New York? You had to be mentally exhausted, because I was?"

"I am, but can't sleep or rest until we find out how your grandmother takes the news and if she'll accept me."

"Sweetheart...either way.... you and I will be happy together, we know the truth, and nothing will keep us apart."

I moved within his reach, we'd been seated across from one another to stretch out, but now I wanted to be close to him. The stars filled the night sky. It was a cold, clear night. When we landed the crispness in the air would mean to bundle up until we arrived at his apartment.

Hopeful Burns had the car warmed up before we climbed in. Mitch and I would have tonight together and tomorrow morning he'd see his grandmother.

Mitch's arm came around me, "I'm really sorry you were unable to nap, you know we need to go out to eat, and it'll be a late night."

Those blue eyes were flashing a warning sign of what was to come later.

We'd be in New York a few days and had tickets for a Broadway show. I wasn't sure where we'd eat tonight we weren't dressed appropriately for fine dining. I thought a New York style pizza at the apartment. I felt the need to unwind.

Mitch was concerned, "Sweetheart, you look worried, unsettled. Are you okay?"

"Too many scenarios are streaming through my head at the moment, Mitch...but we're together. It's all that matters." I had to ask, "Can we do pizza at the apartment?"

He looked at me with a smile, "You want to be alone with me... take advantage of me." He chuckled. "I think it's a great idea." His laughter was warm and he pulled me tightly to him and kissed me.

We landed. Burns was there. The plane taxied to a stop. He stood and waited for the door to open and the steps to appear. His face held a smile... he said hello, and grabbed a few pieces of luggage.

Mitch went out the door first. Took my hand to help me down the stairs. I was glad the car was close, it was cold. He had a way of distracting me... beyond belief. My coat remained on the seat where I'd previously sat and now I wasn't clothed appropriately.

Burns held the car door opened and I slid onto the seat. "I'll grab your coat when I return to the plane for the last piece of luggage." He acknowledged.

I thanked him. The car was warm and the door was closed quickly. Our luggage was placed in the trunk.

I was snuggled close to Mitch... Burns returned to chauffer us.

"Burns, we're headed to the apartment now. I won't need you until tomorrow morning... 11:00 a.m." Mitch informed him.

I smiled.

We'd sleep late.

Chapter 53

The night seemed short and before I knew it the sun was up and gleamed like a brand new penny. Mitch was awake, turned me in his arms, and very softly kissed me. He ran his finger along my cheek, "I guess you know you make me crazy."

"Considering the way our night began and ended you could say... I figured it out, but you tend to make me crazy too." I giggled.

"I never really enjoyed sex much until I met you." He said seriously.

I had to smile, because I never did either.

The moment was over. Mitch moved into his persevere mode.

"Okay, what do you say we shower and then have breakfast? I'll go to visit with my grandmother and I may have Burns bring you to me or I'll come here to collect you. Either way, we're going out afterwards to celebrate once Gran's told the truth."

"Mitch, the necklace your great grandmother wore in the portrait...what do you think happened to it?" I probed.

"I don't know... but we haven't searched the entire secret room for any more than what was in the books. I'll ask her maybe she knows... or even has it." He said.

What remained of the morning I had to myself. My laptop turned on, a few sights in Belize were searched.

Mitch was familiar enough with Belize he'd know where the best place for our ceremony would be. Then I browsed the web for wedding gowns, nothing too fancy for on the beach, but I wanted to wear a gown.

My engagement ring was beautiful and I needed to find a wedding band for Mitch. Perusing the internet, I became drowsy. Still in my robe a nap maybe a good idea. We didn't sleep much… again… last night.

❧

I was shown into her sitting room, "Well, Mitch? To what do I owe the pleasure of this visit?"

"I love you too, grandmother. I don't know why you carry such an attitude since I decided to live in Windward Manor?" He stooped to kiss her hello.

She answered, "You have known most of your life why I hated the place and don't feel the need to repeat myself." She said.

"Well, you'll be surprised when I tell you who Caroline was and what grandfather had to say about you." He stated.

My grandmother's eyes widened and she said, "How would you know?"

"You remember telling me about the secret room? Kristen and I discovered it and among the things tucked away so neatly was a picture of Caroline. Kristen and I searched through 185 years' worth of ledgers and receipts. We found a copy the day and year the artist was commissioned to paint the portrait and it was before grandfather was born."

I could see my grandmother's feathers had been ruffled as

she haughtily said, "I don't believe it for one minute." And rose from her seat.

"Well believe it... because it's true. Come sit down and let me tell you the story behind the painting and how everything you thought all these years wasn't at all the way you assumed." I guardedly began.

She became loud and argumentative... and didn't want to hear what I had to say, she knew in her heart the truth. I asked her again calmly to please take a seat.

From my attaché case I removed the delicate, tattered and yellowed with time paper's displaying the date the artist was commissioned to paint the portrait along with the receipt for its completion. My grandmother hesitated to look at them.

I had to coax her, "Gran, I wouldn't lie to you... you know it to be true, why would you act this way towards me. I want you in my life... in our life with my soon to be wife. Please listen to me."

Once she looked at the dates, and who commissioned the artist... I sensed the tears would come to the surface. After I calmed her the housekeeper was called to bring us a cup of tea. I thought this would help to sooth her.

We sipped tea for a while and she asked in a mild mannered tone, "Who was... Caroline?"

"She was great grandfather's first wife and your husband's mother... my great grandmother. I have grandfather's diary with me, would you like to read it or would you like me to tell you what he's written? By the way, you never told me your family was tenants in the overseer's cottage?"

She looked at me with a sadness I'd never seen from her before. It told me how much she despised where she grew up and must have loved my grandfather for taking her away from such a life. She believed he truly didn't care about her, but only wanted what she could give him, and how much he must have loved Caroline.

My grandmother built a fortress around her heart, refused to allow anyone, but my father, and me in. I needed to change this. I had to, because it was either she accepts Kristen or we wouldn't be the type of family I wanted. I'd have to exclude my grandmother from many special events in my life.

I began to read the letter to my grandfather from his father and then my grandfather's words from his diary. How he'd never known his mother, growing up with a step-mother not mindful why she treated him differently, and how lonely his life was.

"Gran, he said in the diary he sits and waits for your return."

I read it all. She collapsed into tears. She was pulled close to my heart and allowed to cry. Her cries brought tears to my eyes.

She was a proud woman and I've never seen her weep. She'd held those tears in check for many years, never to allow anyone to know how she hurt on the inside.

"Gran...please don't cry, you must stop. I didn't come here to upset you, only to let you know the truth. We're glad we uncovered this evidence for you."

It seemed like forever before she could speak and hold back the flow of tears. I had one, no two questions for her. Really three questions now I think about it.

"Gran, I hope this clears Kristen of any wrong and you accept her as my wife." She wiped at her eyes and looked at me.

"Will you be able to visit Windward Manor?" I challenged.

I handed her my handkerchief she wasn't ready to commit. Then out of curiosity I asked, "Do you have any idea where the necklace would be Caroline wore in the portrait?"

She surprised me when she finally spoke, "I can answer all of your questions. Yes, I can accept Kristen, but must say

I hope my apology is recognized." She continued to wipe at residual tears.

"Not a problem, Gran. She's been upset for you and wanted to resolve this mystery for many years, but never expected me, or to fall in love."

"Mitch, I'm so sorry and yes, I'd like to visit on occasion. And, Mitch, your grandfather gave me the necklace. Even though it belonged to her, it was kept to remind me how much he meant to me. I did him a disservice because I was acrimonious and he died with a broken heart. My heart was broken too, but I'd had your father, and then you. I don't want to drive you away." She beseeched.

She began to cry again, "Will you be able to forgive me?"

I held her tightly and kissed her cheek, "Gran, I only have you and Kristen in my life. I wouldn't know what to do without you. I love you dearly. You were more like my mother than grandmother. Who would I'd be today without you. You've taught me to love, respect, show compassion, and to stand up for what was right. I owe you my life."

Chapter 54

I sat with my grandmother for a while, until she had herself calmed down. I asked if she'd like for me to bring Kristen to her or would she prefer to dine with us this evening.

A smile crossed her face, "Mitch, I may make a fool of myself if we were to dine out. I'd like you to bring Kristen for dinner tonight. Maggie, will cook us a nice meal."

Maggie had been with my grandmother for as long as I could remember and was the part of her staff who cooked. Her food was always a delight and she'd prepared meals for me since I'd been in college. I thought Gran, may be right. To eat here would be more comfortable for her... and for Kristen.

"Gran... I think Kristen and I'd love to eat with you tonight." I took hold of my grandmother and hugged her to me. I had my family back... even though it was small, it was mine.

I said goodbye to my grandmother with the promise I'd see her for dinner and returned to my apartment where I knew Kristen waited for me. There would be good news for her.

I was finally up, dressed, refreshed, and ready for Mitch, with hope we'd go out to lunch since there wasn't much here to prepare what I'd call a significant meal.

Burns dropped me off in front of *The Carlton House*. "Burns, wait here. I want to see if Kristen would like to go to lunch."

I thought if she was dressed we could eat at the Carnegie Deli and walk around midtown Manhattan. It was a long walk to the deli, but would be a quick ride and besides… it was cold.

The door opened into the foyer. I was seated on the sofa reading.

"Mitch?" I queried.

He walked at a fast pace towards me, "It's me sweetheart… you hungry? I thought if you were dressed we'd go to lunch. What do you say?"

I moved to greet him, "I say, hello my love. I'm hungry so it sounds wonderful, and all things with your grandmother must have gone well."

By now we'd reached each other. I was in his arms… his lips pressed to mine in a flood of love, and relief. I drew back, "I must say you had a good morning."

His smile lit up my world, "It was good for all intents and purpose, but was very humbling for my grandmother. I saw her cry for the first time in my life. She is usually so strong willed and stubborn. Of course she was a bit her usual self when I told her about our discovery, but she accepted what I had to say."

"And." I anticipated more.

"And she wants to apologize to you. We're to have dinner with her tonight at 7:00."

My arms were around his waist and I pulled him close, "Oh, Mitch... I don't know what to say."

"Say you're ready to have lunch with me and walk around New York."

I went to the master suite and took my heavy winter coat from the closet along with my scarf and gloves. I was ready.

Mitch waited in the foyer on the phone. I heard him tell Burns we'd be right down.

Burns had the door opened and we slid into the backseat, the heat was on and it felt warm inside. I hadn't asked where we were going and didn't care. This was a marvelous—sunny—but cold day.

Burns let us off in front of the Carnegie Deli. I watched Mitch's smile when he helped me from the car.

"I promised you the next time we were in New York, we'd have a corned beef sandwich, and here we are."

Yes... a big fat pickle and a corned beef sandwich was what he'd promised me.

We stepped into the warmth, took a seat near the back of the deli away from the open and closing of the door. Mitch went to place our order, returned with two sodas, napkins. Then went back to grab our sandwiches.

I saw my plate had an extra pickle.

He laughed and so did I... he knew I'd mentioned how much I loved...fat... kosher pickles.

"Mitch, this looks good, plus I'm absolutely happy it's not turkey." We both had a good laugh.

My first bite said *heaven.* I was going to smell like a New

Yorker from the garlic which would remain on my breath from lunch. I had gum in my wristlet, no worries.

We'd finished our lunch and I asked, "Where to from here. I heard you tell Burns you'd call him later."

"We're going to walk and see some of the shops, Niemen Marcus, Nordstrom and many more... Tiffany's."

He had a smile on his face and we began our walk. The hustle and bustle of New York after Thanksgiving seemed to be more people than when we were here previously.

"Mitch, we walked before, but not in the shopping district. I'd like to look at decorations for our Christmas tree."

"Let's see how much time we have today. I have two places I'd like for you to visit and we can come back tomorrow and shop all day." He said.

We walked swiftly and briskly. It was windy and cold, but refreshing. I was glad to see Mitch feeling better about his grandmother. We stopped in front of 'Angelique Bridal' oh my... the window display was fabulous.

He opened the door and we walked in. There were so many gowns to choose from, they say it's bad luck for the groom to see the bride's gown.

"Mitch, you shouldn't be here with me."

"I know, but thought we could set up an appointment for you and your girlfriends to come back and shop for your gown."

My hands flew to my mouth. It took me a minute before I could say his name.

"Mitch..."

His smile and those eyes sent heat though my body.

"I can work at my New York office, while you and the girls shop. What do you say?" He begged.

"Yes, but I'd have to see when they can take off work."

"It's been taken care of. We needed to see the shop first, it's supposed to be the finest and I have the date… let's see if it will work for their schedule." He said.

Our appointment was set for the 19th of December. Mitch said be ready to leave Thursday evening and my friends and I could shop on Friday while he worked. Burns would be available. We'd leave Sunday evening to return home.

We continued to walk until we came to Tiffany's. Mitch called Burns and told him to give us at least an hour then pick us up in front.. I watched him closely… he ended his call.

"Are we to shop or browse?" I inquired

"Shop, I thought we could get our wedding bands out of the way while we're here. What do you think?" He replied.

I had his hand, but now turned my body towards him to get close to his chest, kissed his cheek and smiled and said, "I think it sounds like a wonderful idea."

My engagement ring was gorgeous, and I'd had no idea what type of band would complete the set, there were so many to choose from. Mitch spoke with a sales person. She went directly to the band which matched my ring.

I looked at him in surprise, "You bought my ring here? I knew it was exquisite, but never expected you bought it here. I'm…lost for words. The band is perfect. I love it. Thank you."

"I wanted to make sure you liked the band before I bought it. They will size it and we can pick it up on the 19th." He responded with a smile.

"Okay, I'm taken care of let's look and see what you might like." I said.

We had it narrowed down to two, the final choice was his. I held my breath hopeful he'd pick the one I liked. He did. It would be sized and ready on the 19th. Now we had the rings… could I wait until February?

Chapter 55

Burns was double parked. We made our escape through the crowd of people on the busy sidewalk. Mitch said we had time before going to his grandmother's for dinner... did I want to change?

Yes. A dress would be more appropriate than slacks.

Burns drove us home.

Both of us changed into a not too casual outfit for our evening with Samantha Savage.

Her home was a brownstone and quite gracious and spacious. We were greeted at the door by a butler. I thought either her husband's will or allowances permitted her most of what she has or her son and grandson helped her reach this pinnacle in life.

We were shown into the library, she appeared immediately. Mitch greeted her with a kiss. I wasn't so sure how to approach her and stepped forward timidly. She extended her hands to reach for mine.

"Kristen, I owe you an apology and also a thank you for what you have helped my grandson discover about... well about my past which led me to believe my husband loved another.

I'm sorry for the way I treated you when Mitch was injured... because I could see with my own eyes how much you loved him. I'm a stubborn old coot, until I'm proven wrong and then... well can you forgive me?" She asked.

There was a display of tears, but I said, "Yes. I forgive you. Will you let me give you a hug? I need a grandmother in my life too."

Her smile was big when she took my hand and led us into the great room. We would have a glass of wine and presumed delicious hors d'oeuvres, since it was all Mitch talked about on our ride here.

A woman dressed as a maid or her housekeeper... brought in the exclusively made specialties Mitch had said were his favorite. Wine was poured and the conversation... was wonderful.

I thought Mitch needed to ask his grandmother about Christmas with us in Windward Manor, but he didn't mention a single word or discuss the wedding in Belize. I knew there had to be a reason... I had no idea why and didn't ask.

Dinner was served and conversation was pleasant. Later we retired into the great room for dessert.

On the ride home I questioned, "Mitch, why didn't you ask your grandmother about Christmas or tell her about the wedding?"

"Kristen, I didn't want to overwhelm her with too much in one day. I'll ask her. I want to give her time to let the truth sink in."

"I knew you had a reason or I'd have interjected in the flow of conversation." I said.

It was midnight when we reached Mitch's home... tired from our walk, and the excitement of the day. We prepared for bed. I laid in Mitch's arms feeling our lives were back on track. Being relaxed and full it wasn't long before I fell asleep wrapped in his love.

His phone rang and woke me. I heard Mitch answer, "Yes Gran, it would be wonderful, we'd love for you to spend the holidays with us. Yes, we'll be back on the 18th. You can return with us when we leave New York for Maryland. Great I'll tell Kristen she'll be happy you've decided to visit."

I leaned on my elbow, "This is fantastic. If only I can get my parents to visit, it will be our first family gathering. I have so many ideas and wanted to talk to you about them, but wasn't sure how your grandmother would react to the news and we've been so busy with the hidden room and ..."

"Calm down sweetheart. I can see you're excited."

"Mitch, I don't have much time to prepare. We'll have Christmas Eve at our home and dinner Christmas Day. There hasn't been a great Christmas in my life for years... really since I left home. We need to invite our family and friends. Would it be alright?"

"Yes, it's alright. I want everyone too." He said.

"We need to shop... we need decorations for trees..." I implored.

"Sweetheart, how many trees do you plan on...?" His facial expression showed fear.

I had to laugh, not sure after he heard what I wanted... what his reaction might be.

"Well, one would look wonderful in the foyer—to greet our

guests. We wouldn't need one in the ball room… but then… it would look bare. How about one in the dining room, the study the great room, and the pub… that's all."

"Okay, but I think there are a few ornaments in the attic and you're right we need to get busy. I'll notify Paul and let him know the size of the crowd. Maybe we're looking at the Thanksgiving crowd plus my grandmother and hopefully your parents. I'll tell him to locate a household staff for the holidays. This may sound crazy, but now you have me excited too."

We were on our way home with tons of decorations, presents, and what we had time to buy. Burns and Katie were with us. Katie and Brittany would handle the shop for me. I wrote list after list of what I wanted and when we reached home Paul and I'd compare notes.

A call to my parents surprised me when told they'd come for Christmas. I was happy for their decision. There was much to be done. I had no idea who on the Eastern Shore would be able to have the house decorated in time.

Mitch made the decision. He hired the company who decorated Rockefeller Center and its tree. If they could handle Rockefeller Center they could handle Windward Manor, he'd said.

Ethan agreed to oversee the projects we wanted completed for the holidays.

Chapter 56

W e were back in New York and Ethan would supervise the Christmas decorations on the inside and outside of our home. I spoke with Mitch's grandmother and asked if she would like to accompany my friends and me on Friday to shop and help select my gown on Saturday. She agreed.

She was older than my mother, but kept up with us. We shopped and went in and out of stores. She had a wonderful sense of humor and life seemed to move in the right direction for both of us.

I was bubbled over with the anticipation of Christmas. Burns would have to bring out the stretch limo to handle all of our wrapped packages.

There wouldn't be time when I arrived home to wrap gifts. Gran said she had a few wonderful holiday cookie recipes and we'd bake upon our arrival to the manor.

She said, "The last time Christmas cookies were baked was before Mitch went off to college. I'm excited to see if I remember how." And she laughed.

Between Jeanette, Ava, and Gran they each had their favorite gown for me to try on. The first one modeled, I saw Gran's eyes cloud over with tears.

I walked to her, "Gran, do you like this one?"

"Kristen, you're so beautiful, it won't make a difference which one you choose. Mitch will be... What's the phrase, *boiled over?*"

I had to laugh and give her a hug.

"Kristen... I can only tell you I see why Kent and my husband both loved Caroline and I realize why Mitch fell in love with you. Your beauty like Caroline's shines through from the inside, I was so stupid..."

"Gran, I'm grateful you're here with me. Be happy... please."

"Okay, I got a bit melancholy. I'm good and yes I love this gown, but try on the others and we'll help you make a decision."

Ava and Jeanette conversed easily and laughed at Gran's jokes. I think the wine, sipped, helped ease any pressure... since everyone got along.

I tried on four gowns.

Of course there was my favorite too. Now it was time to decide. They were told to remember the ceremony would be on a beach, possibly warm, trade winds and sand.

The final decision made and all agreed. It was the strapless gown, with a sweetheart neck, full, but with fluid sheer material. Light and beautiful. Mitch would love this gown.

Gran handed me something she held enclosed in her hand and placed in mine and said, "You can wear this with the gown. Mitch is to put this on you. I'd like you to wear it for your wedding... something old.

I was fascinated with the beauty of the antique piece. She

handed me the box and I laid the specimen to rest again in its case."

I searched her face, "Gran, are you sure about this?"

It was the necklace Caroline wore in the painting. It would be perfect with the gown. Its woven circular weave of white gold, a short cable, not a choker a little longer, with a huge round diamond set in the center. It was magnificent.

I saw the expression on Ava and Jeanette's face. I hadn't the opportunity to tell them the story.

It was time.

On our way back to Gran's I asked if I could tell her story and the mystery which no longer surrounded the manor. She agreed. Jeanette and Ava were stunned... they had no idea the portrait was of Caroline. I told of the mistake Mitch's grandmother made to believe her husband was in love with another woman and was why she disappeared. We delved deeper into the story of the light seen each night as Mitchell kept watch for Samantha's return.

Mitch's grandmother felt better once her story was told.

Gran went home to change. We'd all go to dinner together, Mitch was to be our escort.

Upon our return to the apartment after a gown choice was made, Jeanette and Ava went to change for dinner... Mitch and I went to our room.

He had me engulfed in his arms, "Did you find a gown, sweetheart?"

"I did. It's beautiful. I hope you'll like it Mitch, and Gran wants me to wear her necklace."

I saw the surprise written on his face, "I'm so happy she came around, Kristen. I couldn't endure my life without her, but without you, it would have killed me. Will you wear it?"

"Yes. I want you to place it around my neck."

I handed the box to Mitch. The look of surprise on his face said he didn't expect me to have the jewelry in my possession.

He looked at the piece, removed it from the box, and held it in his hand, "Kristen, I've seen this necklace before."

"Of course you have. Caroline wore it in her portrait."

"Yes... yes I know... I don't know why... it stunned me."

I turned my back to him. He stood behind me. The moment the necklace touched my neck. I felt it... the connection between us, a lost love. It was so strong it shocked me. It was an electrical charge and my hand was raised to touch the choker... Mitch hooked the latch. We were transported back in time.

He kissed my neck and said, "Caroline, wear this as a token of my love."

I turned to look at him... and realized I almost called him, Kent.

"Mitch! What just happened?"

"Oh my God... Kristen... I did this once before."

"Yes we did. I wanted to respond with... "Kent, forever."

"I am Kent Mitchell Savage, but you're Kristen."

I responded with, "Yes, but my middle name is Caroline. Not the same full name... but the same person. Mitch, I knew we'd find each other and destined to live in Windward Manor.. together forever."

"I believe you're right. I said you were my destiny. It was meant to be. Don't tell Gran just yet. I want her to visit and then... we'll see how the house accepts her. Did you tell Ava and Jeanette?" He asked.

Yes. "When, Jeanette and Ava saw the necklace we had to tell the story."

He rubbed his chin, "How did it go over with, Gran?"

"She, told most of the story and it seems she's accepted the fact she'd made a horrible mistake, but wanted to rectify it through us.

Mitch removed the necklace and placed it in the box it had reposed in all these years. I couldn't believe any of this, but understood.

Mitch held me close. "We have a second chance. I love you even more after all this time. Together once again." He sighed.

"I'm so happy Mitch. I knew you were mine... endlessly."

He held me tightly in his arms as if I may disappear from him again.

We heard Jen and Ava in the great room. It was time to return to the now.

A decision was made not to mention our past.

I asked before we left the bedroom, "Mitch, did you remember to pick up the rings?"

"I did and have them in safe keeping until February, when will your gown be ready?"

"Not until after Christmas."

"Good, it will give us a chance to return grandmother and maybe enjoy New Year's Eve in New York."

The kiss which followed the conversation left me breathless.

"Mitch, where will Gran sleep when we go home... and my parents?"

A look of anxiety appeared on his face. "I guess the left wing should have been entirely finished before this."

We broke into laughter and couldn't quite get ourselves together. Once we quieted down we were dressed and ready for dinner.

Chapter 57

Headed home to Claiborne the plane was filled with presents bought for Christmas, but the best present was Gran herself, she'd not been back to Windward Manor since she was nineteen. I knew when she caught her first glimpse of the mansion she'd become distraught.

In bed last night Mitch and I made the decision he'd walk his grandmother through the front door of what was to have been her home so many years ago. We wondered what would become of the light in the room where Mitchell kept his nightly lookout for Samantha's return.

We'd landed at BWI and were on our way home. Paul was to have a meal ready when we arrived. Ethan, Alex and Cory were to join us. Of course Burns wanted to get home. He declined dinner.

Mitch drove the five of us from the airport and Burns drove the stretch limo, which had been arranged for the wrapped gifts to be brought to the manor.

The house appeared only slightly lit on approach to the circular drive. We drew nearer to the front of the glorious yet gracious Windward Manor. The outside became ignited with numerous lights and the inside became cheerfully lit in a welcome—like the evening I was lured into the house.

Candles in each window, trees aglow inside, seen from outside. I heard Gran inhale in reverence.

Burns was out of the limo to open the door on Mitch's car for his grandmother. She stood in reticence until we all exited the car.

Mitch held delicately to his grandmother's arm, led her up the steps to the front door, it should have been opened by one of our newly hired household staff... but seemed to open of its own accord. I lagged behind and asked Burns to call if the light was out in the room... when he reached his home.

Cory ran and was breathless with excitement to greet her mom. "Mom, all the lights came on like magic."

Ethan and Alex appeared to greet Jeanette and Ava. I sensed Ethan was about to say something.

"Funny thing, it was quiet, and peaceful with just the perfect, tranquil sort of glow from the tree lights, and candles... when out of the blue every single light in the entire house became lit. The butler didn't get to the door when it opened... this house is..."

I spoke softly and gave a slight chuckle, "I know, Ethan, Jeanette will tell you about it later."

Everyone was introduced. We entered the great room for wine before dinner. I wish my parents could have joined us earlier than the day before Christmas, but with Gran becoming settled, Mitch and I both could be of help to her emotional state.

The dinner bell sounded. We made our way into the dining room. Mitch's phone rang. He answered.

"Sir, I see the light."

"Okay… thanks, Burns. Let me know if the situation changes."

I wasn't quite sure what was said by Mitch's eye contact with me.

When we were seated he whispered, "The light is on."

I found this odd after the hypothesis it would go out for good. The spirit was happy to see us when all the lights came on. I wonder what happened?

Dinner was good as usual. After our meal we made our way into the great room when Gran said she wished to see Mitchell's rooms. Mitch and I must have looked surprised.

He couldn't help but suggest, "Gran, why don't you relax and wait until tomorrow?"

"I need to reconcile with your grandfather… the sooner the better. From what Kristen and you have said he's waited for my return. I'm here now and want to ask his forgiveness for being young and stupid. To think my son could have grown up here, known his father and you… your grandfather. It's time to own up to my mistakes and regrets. Mitchell needs to finally be at peace. I can at least do this much for him."

"Gran, would you like me to come with you?"

"No, Mitch. I'd like to be alone with him."

Gran left us in wonder. We let her go. She knew this house well…. she'd first been a domestic here. I hoped she wouldn't be too hard on herself.

Only moments passed since she'd gone upstairs when

Mitch's phone rang, it was Burns. He said the soft glow of light had disappeared. It was unusual for the room to darken before 1:00 a.m., but hopes had been the glow would extinguish upon her arrival.

We'd give Gran time. If she wasn't downstairs within the next half hour, we'd check on her.

Happy to be home, the decorations, and house looked whimsical, magical and like Christmas. We could hear Jeanette and Ava explain to Ethan and Alex the house's mystery, while Cory laid on the rug near the fireplace with her crayons, and coloring book.

Mitch and I hadn't been in the upstairs of the left wing since the contractors had finished for the holidays. We weren't sure what had been done in the bathrooms or other bedrooms since Mitchell's room was to be painted first and his furniture replaced.

It had been a half hour. We slipped away from the group to check on Gran. The wing appeared to be finished except for the furniture to be placed back in each of the bedrooms, the bathrooms turned out beautifully. We continued down the hall, and peered into Mitchell's room. Grandmother was asleep on his bed.

Mitch spoke softly, "Gran, why don't you let us show you to your room if you're ready for bed?"

"I want to stay here. I'll be fine. Would you have my things brought up... I want to stay where I can feel his presence... please. I'm at home in this room."

"Grandmother, are you sure? We have a bedroom for you in the center of the house."

"I'm very sure… and Kristen, don't forget tomorrow we'll bake cookies. I hope Paul has the pantry filled with baking needs."

Mitch returned with her luggage. I brought fresh linens, blankets, towels, and bathroom necessities upstairs.

Gran didn't want help as she prepared the bed with linens and said, "I'm used to making Mitchell's bed… the way he liked."

After a goodnight kiss was given to each of us we left her to herself hopeful she wouldn't regress into her past life—but happy to be home.

Epilogue

Gran and I baked cookies as planned. Mom and dad came the day before Christmas and left before New Year's Eve.

The family did wonderful together and the mystery of the manor was revealed.

Gran wanted to go home and asked Mitch to make sure when she died... she'd be buried next to her husband.

We hadn't realized the family burial plot was located among the fifteen acres in an isolated gated piece of ground. Gran found it, she must have known where it was since she was a young girl.

It seemed Thomas Mitchell and Elizabeth were buried side by side as husband and wife, Adeline was not buried next to Kent Mitchell and no one knew where Caroline had been buried. And of course Mitchell was for now... buried alone.

Mitch and I made the decision not to offer up the fact we'd been together in our past life. The mystery itself was enough for everyone to digest... why freak them out. We knew... and life would continue.

The wedding in Belize was romantic and beautiful. To have our friends with us for the two weeks was more fun than we would have anticipated, but we had plenty of alone time.

Now the weather turned warm and the May planned reception was about to commence. The flowers were in bloom, the sky was clear, beautiful, the grass lush, and green.

The sun shone its magical light on our day of celebration. The bay gave off a luster from the sun's rays... the reception with family and friends would give us a renewed lifetime of happiness.